"You'll father my baby?"

He nodded. "But we do it my way, on my terms, or not at all." Kat looked directly at her. "First of all, we get married."

"Married!" Emily stared at him, openmouthed.

"Married. As in old shoes, rice, orange blossoms. Married. As in legitimate mother and father for our child."

Emily didn't like the emphasis he'd put on *our*, but she hadn't recovered enough to retaliate.

"Second, I won't agree unless the baby is conceived the old-fashioned way."

Dear Reader,

May is the perfect month to stop and smell the roses, and while you're at it, take some time for yourself and indulge your romantic fantasies! Here at Harlequin American Romance, we've got four brand-new stories, picked specially for *your* reading pleasure.

Sparks fly once more as Charlotte Maclay continues her wild and wonderful CAUGHT WITH A COWBOY! duo this month with *In a Cowboy's Embrace*. Join the fun as Tasha Reynolds falls asleep in the wrong bed and wakes with Cliff Swain, the very *right* cowboy!

This May, flowers aren't the only things blossoming—we've got two very special mothers-to-be! When estranged lovers share one last night of passion, they soon learn they'll never forget *That Night We Made Baby*, Mary Anne Wilson's heartwarming addition to our WITH CHILD... promotion. And as Emily Kingston discovers in Elizabeth Sinclair's charming tale, *The Pregnancy Clause*, where there's a will, there's a baby on the way!

There's something fascinating about a sexy, charismatic man who seems to have it all, and Ingrid Weaver's hero in *Big-City Bachelor* is no exception. Alexander Whitmore has two wonderful children, money, a successful company.... What could he possibly be missing...?

With Harlequin American Romance, you'll always know the exhilarating feeling of falling in love.

Happy reading!

Melissa Jeglinski
Associate Senior Editor

The Pregnancy Clause

ELIZABETH SINCLAIR

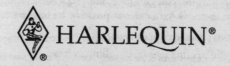

HARLEQUIN®

TORONTO • NEW YORK • LONDON
AMSTERDAM • PARIS • SYDNEY • HAMBURG
STOCKHOLM • ATHENS • TOKYO • MILAN • MADRID
PRAGUE • WARSAW • BUDAPEST • AUCKLAND

ISBN 0-373-16827-6

THE PREGNANCY CLAUSE

Copyright © 2000 by Marguerite Smith.

Visit us at www.eHarlequin.com

Printed in U.S.A.

ABOUT THE AUTHOR

Elizabeth Sinclair was born and raised in the scenic Hudson Valley of New York State. In 1988 she and her husband moved to their present home in St. Augustine, Florida, where she began pursuing her writing career in earnest. Her first novel reached #2 on the Waldenbooks bestseller list and won a 1995 Georgia Romance Writers' Maggie Award for Excellence. As a proud member of five RWA affiliated chapters, Elizabeth has taught creative writing and given seminars and workshops at both local and national conferences on romance writing, how to get published, promotion and writing a love scene and the dreaded synopsis.

Books by Elizabeth Sinclair

HARLEQUIN AMERICAN ROMANCE

Don't miss any of our special offers. Write to us at the following address for information on our newest releases.

Harlequin Reader Service
U.S.: 3010 Walden Ave., P.O. Box 1325, Buffalo, NY 14269
Canadian: P.O. Box 609, Fort Erie, Ont. L2A 5X3

ROSE'S BAKED FRENCH TOAST

1 *loaf white bread, cubed*
8 *oz cream cheese, cubed*
8-12 *eggs, depending on size*
$1/2$ *cup maple syrup*
1 *cup milk*

Using a 11x13-inch pan, line the bottom with
$1/2$ of the bread cubes. Next, layer the cream
cheese on top of the bread. Then add the
remaining bread cubes on top. Beat the eggs,
maple syrup and milk together. Pour entire
mixture over bread. Cover and refrigerate
overnight. Bake at 350°F for 45 minutes or until
lightly golden brown.

Serves 8

Chapter One

"You must have a baby before you turn thirty or Clover Hill Farms will be turned over to charity."

A baby? In ten and a half months?

Twenty-nine-year-old Emily Kingston stared in awe across the highly-polished mahogany desk into the somber face of the young lawyer. Lawrence Tippens recited the conditions of the codicil to her father's five-year-old will as if he'd just told her to put on fresh lipstick.

"Why didn't someone tell me this five years ago, when my father's will was read?" She felt her eyes widen. "If I have a baby that means I have to...to..."

A red blush suffused Lawrence's face. "Yes, well, the codicil doesn't stipulate *how* you have the child, only that you have one by the time you turn thirty."

Despite this emotional upset, Emily had to hide a smile. Lawrence would never change. He was as much a prude now as when he was in high school.

"Now, as to why you weren't told about the codicil at the reading of the primary will—'' He brushed imaginary lint from his navy, pin-striped lapels and avoided her gaze. Obviously, he hadn't counted on her asking about the delay in the notification, or he'd hoped that she wouldn't ask for details. ''I regret to say that my father's memory wasn't too acute in his last years, and he did not employ the best filing system. In fact…ahem…he didn't really have a system to speak of at all. He did most of his work at home and failed to transfer it to his town office so his secretary could put it in the proper place.''

Emily leaned toward the embarrassed man. ''Exactly what are you trying to tell me, Larry?''

He bristled at the use of the nickname. ''Last week, while cleaning out the closet in my father's home office, my mother found a box of legal papers. My secretary discovered the codicil in that box. Since my father passed away only a week after your father, I doubt anyone knew about the codicil other than the two of them. As it was, if you recall, because my father was so gravely ill at the time, it took two weeks to locate the original will.''

''But this doesn't make sense. When my father told me about the terms of his will, he gave me the impression that I would have sole ownership of Clover Hill Farms. He never said anything about a baby or the farm reverting to charity.''

Lowering his wire-rimmed spectacles to the bridge of his bony nose, Lawrence stared at her. ''I cannot speak to your father's reasoning or his decision. I can only relate what the codicil says. The terms of the original will were just as you say. The farm went solely to you—however, the codicil changes all that.''

Emily shook her head. ''I don't understand any of this.''

The young lawyer sighed impatiently. ''Let me explain.'' Lawrence straightened the papers on his desk, lining them up like soldiers at a dress parade. ''When your father originally had my father draw up his will, the terms were as you've stated them. This codicil applies conditions to that original document and to your continued ownership. You must meet these terms in the allotted time or lose the horse-breeding farm to the charity your father has designated here as his new beneficiary.'' He used his forefinger to push his glasses back in place, then shuffled through the papers. ''The Horseman's Benevolent Association.''

Emily sighed, leaned back, then took a deep fortifying breath. The smell of lemon oil, leather-bound books, stale smoke and Larry's expensive, overpowering, cologne assaulted her. The combination turned her already queasy stomach. ''Is it legal? Could he do that?''

''Yes, he had every right to put additional stipulations on the distribution of his estate. I'm afraid you will have to produce a child in ten and a half months or you'll lose your horse farm.'' He cleared his throat. ''Of course, I'm sure he assumed that marriage would precede the blessed event.''

''That's impossible.'' Emily wasn't about to tie herself to any man.

He eyed her over his glasses, his gesture making him look older than his thirty years. "You mean you don't have a young man who's pressing you to marry?" Lawrence leered. "Of course, you didn't date all that frequently in high school, but you've turned into an attractive woman. There must be men lined up on your porch." His leer deepened. "If I can be of any help with the...uh...baby problem, don't hesitate to ask."

His condescending tone caused Emily's anger to churn inwardly. Whatever made this pompous ass think she'd resort to asking him to father her child? She'd spent four years in high school avoiding his amorous overtures. Why would she change her mind now? Not in this lifetime. She'd rather walk over hot coals than climb into bed with Lawrence Tippens.

And as far as her personal life went, she wasn't about to share with this stodgy legal machine that the Sahara Desert had a better chance of getting a torrential rain than she did of getting a date. She couldn't be expected to run a business like hers and still play the social butterfly. The only nursery she should be planning to furnish should be one with hay on the floor.

"Thanks but no thanks, Larry. This idea needs getting used to. I'm a horse breeder—I'm not cut out to be a mother."

He bristled at her rejection, just as he'd done in high school, then became all business again. "Am I to assume then that you're willing to let the farm go to charity?"

"No, certainly not." The smug—Emily fought to remember she was a lady.

"In that case, short of contesting this, I see no other alternative for you except to comply."

A dim ray of hope rose in Emily. "Contesting? You mean I can fight this legally?"

"You can." Lawrence jogged the papers, papers that had changed her life, into a neat stack, then returned them to the manila folder from which he'd taken them a half hour ago. "However, since your father was of sound mind, your chances of winning are slim at best."

Standing, Emily walked to the window overlooking the main street of the small town of Bristol, New York. She'd lived here all her life. Everyone knew everyone, along with their business. The thought of having to face people with the news of what had gone on here today made her want to crawl off in a corner and hide. And it would spread beyond these doors, she had no doubt. Larry could never keep a juicy little tidbit like this to himself.

A movement in the windowpane drew her attention from the lazy activity of Main Street. Reflected in the window, she could see Larry fingering a cigar, no doubt in anticipation of her leaving. He was much too proper to light it with her there, but the stale smell of predecessors to the cigar he held already clung to the legal books and drapes. Little did he realize that the cigar didn't fit his professional personae any more than being a mother fit hers.

She knew nothing about raising babies. What could her father have been thinking? Larry had described Frank Kingston as being of sound mind. An arguable description from her standpoint.

She shouldn't be shocked at this turn of events. Frank Kingston had either been breaking promises to her, her sister Honey and her brother Jesse all their lives or running other people's lives. He'd known how much the breeding farm meant to her. He'd promised it would be hers. *Hers.* Why the change of heart? She shook her head. It didn't make sense.

However, little her father did made sense to those not privy to his reasoning. Sense or no sense, he'd trapped her by making it all very legal and very binding. *Men!* They just couldn't be trusted. Hadn't she figured that one out a long time ago?

"If you have no further questions...." Lawrence stood and walked around his desk, obviously anxious to get rid of her.

"No. I think that's quite enough for one day."

As Emily made her way across the thick carpet to the door, she decided that her opinion of Lawrence hadn't changed since high school. He was a pompous windbag of a man, so full of himself and his profession that she doubted there was room left over for a heart inside his bony chest. Nothing like his gregarious, soft-spoken father.

Emily halfheartedly shook the hand he offered, then left the cigar-scented offices of Tippens, Tippens and Forge.

As KAT Madison watched out the café window, a young woman, obviously intent on something other than her safety, walked into the street and was nearly run down by an oncoming car. She looked familiar. That he couldn't place her from this distance didn't stop him from appreciating the gentle sway of her single dark braid against her denim-encased hips or the swell of her breasts beneath a white T-shirt shouting in black letters, I've Got The Answers.

Lucky her. Finding answers had brought him home to Bristol for the first time in over sixteen years, since his parents' funeral. He'd only stayed for a day. Thoughts of that day drove a pain through his heart. Out of habit, he pushed them to the back of his mind.

"More coffee?"

Kat glanced at the young blonde he'd been flirting outrageously with before spotting the T-shirt-clad woman across the street. Nodding, he turned his gaze back to the street in time to see her red pickup drive by the window, heading out of town. Across the truck's door in white letters he read Clover Hill Farms.

Emily?

Just his luck to be ogling the one person he really wasn't ready to come face-to-face with. The one person who would inevitably confront him with questions he couldn't answer.

"Here's the key."

Dave Thornton's deep voice roused Kat from his observations. "Thanks." He took the key to the summer cottage his friend had arranged for Kat to use until he found somewhere to live.

"I told the power company that you'd call when

you leave so they can cut off the electric. Oh, and I had the phone turned on, too.''

"Thanks." Kat shook the key. "I owe you one."

Dave smiled. "So, what do you plan on doing with your parents' house, Kat? Or do you go by Rian now?''

Kat wanted to correct him, but for all intents and purposes, Hilda and Charlie Madison had been his parents. Were still his parents. Besides, what other name could he use?

He shrugged. "Kat's fine."

He fell silent, remembering how his father had come up with the nickname because of his son's ability to enter and leave a room without being noticed, a trait that had proven helpful on more than one occasion.

Stirring his coffee, Dave grimaced. "I'm sorry. I guess you don't want to talk about them, huh?''

Kat laid a hand on his friend's shoulder. "It's been sixteen years since they died in the fire."

"I know, but when you love someone, it's hard to forget."

The sharp pain of their death had dulled with time. What hadn't diminished was the pain brought on by what he'd found the day he'd sifted through the ashes of the partially burned house. He wondered if that ache would ever fade—or if he'd get any answers.

Dave stood. "Well, I gotta run. I promised Marilyn I'd meet her and go wallpaper shopping." He grinned. "We're turning the spare room into a nursery."

Kat grabbed Dave's extended hand and shook it, feeling envy eat at him. "Hey, congratulations, Dad. Thanks again. Say hello to Marilyn for me."

"Will do." Dave waved and slipped out the door.

Kat watched Dave leave the café. He hadn't changed since high school. Tall, lanky and devoted to the woman he'd loved exclusively since seventh grade, Dave had found happiness, happiness compounded by the addition of a child. Lucky devil.

For a moment Kat allowed the envy to seep in, before he stopped it with a reminder that he was here to rebuild his parent's house and sell it, not to form relationships. He had other things to settle first. Wives, homes and babies would have to wait their turn.

Throwing some change on the counter, he smiled at the blonde, then headed for his car. If he was going to rebuild the house, he might as well bite the bullet and take a look at it to figure out what he was going to need in the way of building supplies.

A BABY.

Emily had been pacing her living room and repeating those two words for over an hour, but full comprehension of her father's demand still hadn't registered. Why had he done this to her? If only Rose were here. Having been with the family for nearly sixteen years and having acted as Emily's father's sounding board, Rose knew better than most why Frank Kingston had done things.

Fine time for Emily's housekeeper cum maternal confidant to be somewhere in Mexico touring pyramid ruins with her friends. Emily's mother had died when Emily was a teenager and Rose was the closest thing to a mother that she had now. She'd gotten used to talking through her problems with Rose. Rose had more logic in her little finger than most people had in their whole heads, even if she was a bit on the old-fashioned side.

Emily nearly had this self-pity thing down to a fine art when the doorbell rang. The last thing she wanted right now was company. Cautiously, she peeked through the side window, then swung open the door.

"Hey, sister." Honey and her four-year-old son Danny smiled at Emily from the front porch.

Pushing between his mother and his aunt, Danny tugged on Emily's shirttail. "Aunt Emily, c-c-can I go s-s-see the horsies?" Danny's eyes glowed with excitement.

"*May* I, Danny." Honey frowned at her son. "And it would be nice if you said hello before you start making your aunt crazy."

"Aw, Mommy." Danny rolled his eyes at his mother, but adoration shone from his gaze.

For the first time, Emily thought about the baby her father insisted she have as something other than a complication she didn't need in her life right now. How bad would it be to have a little person like Danny to look at you with love, trust and honesty?

"Hello, Aunt Emily. Now, c-c-can I go s-s-see the horsies?"

Honey sighed and shook her head. "The child is going to grow up illiterate despite my best efforts."

Another, more insistent tug on her shirt drew Emily's attention back to her nephew. His stutter hadn't gotten any better. She'd hoped that time would ease his grief over his father's death, and his stutter would go away, as the doctor had predicted. So far, it wasn't working.

Emily scooped his sturdy body up into her arms. The feel of him cuddled to her chest made her suddenly aware of how good it felt to hold a child close, to inhale that special child-fragrance. "Sure you *can,* sweetie. Just stay out of the stalls, do as Chuck says and don't get too near the mommy horsies, okay? But it's gonna cost you." She tapped her cheek with a blunt nail. "Plant one right there."

Danny grinned and bestowed a wet kiss to her upturned cheek. She set him back on his feet. Without hesitation, he scampered down the steps, then raced in the direction of the barn. Emily watched him, her heart assuming a strange new beat.

Honey sighed. "The child is incorrigible."

"You worry too much about how he's going to grow up. He's a good kid. He'll be fine."

"I plan on making certain of that. Speaking of fine, will he be okay out there?"

Emily nodded. "Chuck will keep an eye on him. He loves having Danny around." She continued to watch as Danny's short legs carried him to the barn. "And you can stop worrying about him. He'll make a fine man some day."

"Well, you don't help matters when you—" Honey leaned into Emily's line of vision. "Do I see maternal longing in those green eyes?"

Emily straightened and glared at her sister. Sometimes the closeness they had was more of a liability than a blessing. Maybe if she just ignored her.... "Did you come over here just to antagonize me or is there another purpose for your visit?" She walked into the house ahead of Honey, leading her into the kitchen. "Coffee?"

Honey feigned a look of horror. She backed up, as if to escape some threat. "What terrible thing have I done to be subjected to a cup of that black poison you call coffee?"

Smiling for the first time today, Emily waved her into a chair and got a can of soda for each of them from the refrigerator. Honey could always cheer her up. "Okay, so I can't make coffee to save my life. Shoot me. With Rose around, I don't need culinary talents."

"Em, you may be an ace with those four-legged beasts you love, but you wouldn't know a culinary talent if it bit you on the backside." Honey popped the can, tucked a wayward strand of her long, blond hair behind her ear, then took a sip. "When's Rose due back?"

"Not for a while. About two weeks, I think." Sighing, Emily looked around the sparkling yellow kitchen. "If someone doesn't take pity on me, I just may starve to death before then. One can survive for just so long on peanut butter and banana sandwiches."

Honey snickered at her younger sister's blatant bid for a dinner invitation. "You sure picked the wrong night to wangle a dinner invitation. Tess is making her prizewinning meat loaf tonight. Now, if you'd waited until tomorrow night, Tess has it off and I man the kitchen.'' She curled her nose. ''But I don't dare go near it while Tess is there.''

''It's a good thing the woman has a day off, or I'd worry more about Danny's nutrition than his manners.'' She shook her head. ''I'll never understand why your mother-in-law has kept her for all these years. Amanda can certainly afford someone better.''

Honey shrugged. ''Tess grows on you.''

''So does bacteria, but most people don't encourage it.'' Tess made the only gray meat loaf Emily had ever seen in her life. She wasn't a cook by any means, but even she knew meat loaf should be brown.

Avoiding Emily's comment, Honey took a sip from her soda can.

Lowering her voice as if she might be overheard, Emily leaned toward Honey. ''Wonder where she won that prize, and how many drinks the judges had before they awarded it to her.''

Honey snickered. ''Never mind where she won it. If hers was the winner, can you imagine what the losers were like?''

Both women laughed.

''So, what does bring you here, aside from being thrown out of Amanda's kitchen by a woman small enough to have learned how to cook in a hollow tree with a bunch of elves?''

''Just plain nosiness.'' Honey set her soda can down. ''What did Tippens want to see you for?''

Emily's good mood evaporated. She rose, then walked to the trash and deposited her empty can. "It seems Dad's will had a codicil." She turned to her shocked sister.

"A codicil? Can they do that? I mean, so long after the will has been read?"

"From what Lawrence said, it can be done any time the deceased requests it be done. Apparently, due to a filing glitch, the codicil was just discovered."

"But how can something like that get misplaced?"

Emily glanced at her. "Larry said his father's filing system left a lot to be desired." Grabbing another soda from the refrigerator, Emily popped the top. Gas hissed from the can. "It gets better. Seems Dad insisted that if I'm to keep Clover Hill Farms, I have to have a baby."

"A baby?" Honey's lower jaw dropped. "And if you don't?"

"If I don't, the farm goes to the Horseman's Benevolent Association."

"What? Well, that sucks dead canaries." Honey leaned forward and rested her forearms on the pine table. "What in blazes possessed Dad to do such a thing?"

"Beats me. But when did he ever not make a sharp left when everyone else was ready to go right?" Throwing herself back in the chair facing her sister, Emily rubbed at the ache in her temple. "He promised me sole ownership of the farm. Why did he lie to me, Honey?"

Honey laughed derisively, took a sip of her soda, then shook her head. "Heaven only knows. Why did he do half the things he did? Why did he insist I marry a man I didn't love? Why did he alienate his own son?" She rose and walked to the window. Pulling the curtain aside, she looked out, presumably checking on Danny's whereabouts. "Everyone in this valley knows that Frank Kingston was a law unto himself. That he left the farm to you came as a surprise to no one, considering that I detest horses and Jesse detested Dad." She shook her head. "He wasn't well-liked, but he sure was obeyed. I figure that Henry Tippens died of that heart attack so quickly after Dad died only because Dad was up there already and poor Henry didn't dare keep him waiting."

Despite Honey's attempt at levity, Emily knew her sister still felt the pain of their father's interference in her life. When he'd insisted Honey marry to make her unborn child legitimate and preserve the Kingston's good name, he'd sentenced his daughter to a life with a man who suffered from a Peter Pan complex. The best thing Stan Logan ever did for Honey and Danny was get himself killed last year in a motorcycle accident. Since then, Honey had made it her life's mission to make sure Danny didn't follow in his father's footsteps.

Emily's father hadn't cared that he'd forced Honey to marry the wrong man. He just didn't want the whole valley to laugh at him. Emily had never mentioned any of this to Honey. Aside from the fact that Honey didn't seem to want to talk about it, Emily had promised her father she would never tell Honey just how much she knew about Danny and his father. To Emily, a promise was golden. Once made, it could not be broken.

She laughed to herself. Frank Kingston had been dead for five years and ironically, he was still running their lives from his grave.

"This may not be as bad as we think." Honey had left the window and returned to her seat across from Emily. "Since you are going to marry sometime, it follows that you'll have children, too. Right?"

"In theory that works, but I didn't tell you the whole thing." She glanced at her sister's raised eyebrow. "I have to have the baby before I turn thirty. Since I just turned twenty-nine, that gives me exactly one and a half months to get pregnant."

Honey let out a long breath. "Hells bells."

"Of course, there's the small problem of finding a man before then." Emily smoothed the corner of the lacy doily in the center of the table. "That is, if I even want a man in my life to begin with."

Honey's laughter filled the kitchen. "I hate to tell you this, little sister, but it's gonna be damned difficult to have that baby without a man."

Emily placed both palms on the table and stared at her sister. "Honey, I can't be a mother. I have no idea what to do with a baby. I don't even know which end to diaper. I didn't even help you take care of Danny when he was small."

"Well, that would have been a little hard, considering I was traveling all over the United States from car race to car race with Stan. And as far as taking care of a baby goes, it's an inborn instinct. Oh, and by the way, you diaper the end with no hair.''

"Cute, Honey. Really cute. I'm at a crossroads in my life and you're making jokes."

"Sorry." Honey didn't look contrite.

Emily stared at her sister. Maybe for some women mothering was inborn, but for Emily, the only babies she had any acquaintance with had four legs and a mane, and not a one of them grew up and attended college or got the measles or...or called her Mommy.

THE NEXT DAY, Emily settled more comfortably on her horse's back. She did her best thinking in the saddle, and she planned on riding out to the west pasture, just to clear her head.

As she rode farther from home, hammering coming from the old Madison place disturbed the silence. She couldn't imagine who would be hammering over there. It had been deserted since fire had partially destroyed it years ago.

She reigned in Butternut and walked him through the barrier of trees dividing her property from the Madisons'. The hammering stopped, replaced by the loud squeak of a rusty nail being torn from old, dry wood. Pushing the branch of a maple out of her way, she peered through at the ruins of the house.

On a ladder, shirtless and bronzed from exposure to the sun, was a man. With one hand he held on to the ladder, while with the other he tore off a half-burned board.

She eased the horse closer. When she was within shouting distance, she stopped.

"What do you think you're doing?"

Surprised, the man spun toward her, almost losing his balance. As he clutched the rung of the ladder, the muscles in his shoulders and arms danced under his tan skin. Butternut sidestepped and a shaft of bright sunlight blinded her from seeing the intruder clearly.

"I would have thought that after all these years, you'd have given up trying to send me to an early grave."

Taken aback by his words and the familiar tone of his voice, Emily eased the horse closer. "Who told you you could tear this house apart?"

"I did. I own it, Squirt. Or have you forgotten?"

Squirt?

Emily sucked in her breath. Only one person in her entire life had called her Squirt, and he'd walked out on her without a word sixteen years ago. Gently nudging Butternut in the ribs, Emily moved into the shadow of an overhanging maple tree to see him more clearly.

Shock ebbed over her. Above his left eyebrow, just below a wayward lock of wavy, jet-black hair, a pencil-thin, two-inch scar marred his tanned skin. She knew that scar very well—after all, she'd been the cause of the injury that had produced it. When she was seven and he was eleven, she'd dared him to jump from the maple in her front yard with a homemade bedsheet parachute. Because he always did anything she asked of him, Kat Madison had jumped and landed facedown on a piece of glass in the driveway.

Kat, the only man she knew who could enter a room and not be heard. She might have known that, true to his nickname, he'd sneak back into town on silent feet. She recalled hearing the story of how he'd insisted on spelling his name with a K to make himself unique. He was unique all right, a unique jerk who cared nothing about a friend's feelings.

Silently, the rhythm of her erratic heart pounding in her ears, she continued to study him. He'd changed. Matured. She quickly did the math in her head. Thirty-three. But more than his age had altered. The lanky Kat she'd known hadn't had muscles out to here and skin the color of soft suede. Nor had that Kat ever looked at her with a mixture of longing and pain in his eyes.

She called her emotions under control, then hardened herself to say all the things she'd been waiting to tell him. Instead, the pain generated by his abrupt appearance spoke for her.

"Were you ever going to tell me you were here or were you going to just walked away again without a word?"

He said nothing. She fought back the sudden rush of tears unaccountably choking her. Turning the horse, she started to ride away, then pulled up short and glanced back.

"You could at least have written." Her voice harsh with emotion, she stared into his dark eyes. Although his face twisted, he said nothing, offered no explanation, made no apologies. "Stay away from me, Kat Madison. Just…stay away."

Quickly, before he could reply, she rode away, her skin cooled by the wind mixing with the tears streaming down her cheeks.

Chapter Two

Kat stood in the reception area of the office of J. R. Pritchard and Associates, Private Investigations. He glanced around at the plush carpeting, the silk foliage, the gleaming chrome-and-leather furniture and the fancy door with the brass plate declaring the room beyond to be Private. Quite a contrast to the drab, grungy offices of the private investigators in the old Humphrey Bogart flicks Kat loved.

"Can I help you?" The curvaceous redhead behind the desk smiled up at him.

Yesterday, Kat would have smiled back, taking advantage of and pleasure in the obvious interest in the woman's eyes. Why not now? His answer came with all the ease of morning turning to night.

Emily.

Their earlier meeting remained fresh in his mind. So fresh, that, even after a shower, he could still feel the dust stirred up by Emily's horse's hooves abrading his sweat-soaked skin. But the discomfort of the grit seemed a fitting cover for the pain inside. He'd lost the friendship of a person who had been a primary player in his young life, his confidant. The image of Emily's pained expression was burned into his conscience.

"Sir?" The receptionist, eyebrow raised, captured Kat's attention. "Did you want to see someone?"

"I have a three o'clock appointment to see Mr. Pritchard."

The woman ran a bloodred nail down her appointment book. "Mr. Madison?"

"Yes."

"Mr. Pritchard has someone in the office with him right now. If you'll take a seat, he'll be with you in a few minutes." She smiled and batted long, false, sooty lashes at him.

"Thanks." Kat turned away, deliberately taking a seat behind the large silk tree that blocked the view of the receptionist.

Once more, his rebellious mind centered on the woman who'd ridden away from him—looking like a part of her horse—a few hours ago. *Woman.* Equating the Emily on that horse with the girl-child he'd left behind sixteen years ago reminded him of his reasons for leaving and for not telling her he was going. Back then, he couldn't have withstood the pain in her eyes any better than he had today.

He admitted he owed her an explanation, but giving her one was a whole different ball game. How could he explain that, sixteen years ago, in the space of a few hours, the life he'd always known had fallen apart? Would she understand that he'd had to find out who he was, get answers, and that those answers lay somewhere beyond the village of Bristol? Would she care that he hadn't found those answers, but that he'd made peace with all that and had come home to stay? Probably not. Their earlier meeting proved conclusively that he'd put the last bullet into the special friendship he and Emily had shared.

A persistent question niggled at the edges of his mind. If he'd made peace with all that, why was he here looking to hire a P.I.? Because the answers to *all* the questions didn't matter anymore. Only the answer to one. *Why?* And only that one because he was curious. Curious as to why his birth parents had left him and allowed him to be adopted by the Madisons.

Kat picked up a glossy magazine, leafed through it then tossed it aside. The fragrance of the receptionist's perfume wafted to him. Its flowery scent brought to mind an image of his adoptive mother. With that image came more, until he could no longer keep the memories at bay.

In his mind, he stepped through the half-removed doorway and into the house in which he'd grown up, the house where he'd known love, laughter and the warmth of a family…until sixteen years ago. He climbed the stairs to their bedroom.

Slowly, memories of the day he'd come home after his parents' funeral crowded his mind. Their room had been untouched by the fire. The closet door hung open, just as it had back then. Sitting on the floor…

Unwilling to get into reliving the day his life had exploded around him, he shook away the memories and strode to the office window. He squinted his eyes against the glare of the bright June sunshine blanketing the city of Albany, New York.

Taking refuge where he had so many times over the years, he thought about Emily. The way his insides always warmed when she smiled at him. The way the mischief in that smile forecast one of her schemes, a scheme that would include him and would inevitably end in disaster. Emily, with tears in her eyes, asking him to help her bury a stillborn kitten or understand why her father had broken another promise. The cool smoothness of her lips on his cheek the day he gave her a necklace for her thirteenth birthday to mark her transition from child to teenager.

He'd told her the tiny gold key suspended from the delicate chain represented the key to their friendship. But after he'd found himself alone and miles away, he'd wondered if it had been the key to something more.

Today, that old magnetism connecting them had tugged at his heart. Back then he'd have coaxed a smile from Emily, but today he'd had to watch her pain and do nothing. Now, instead of using their friendship as a refuge, they'd been on the outside, both of them, for their own reasons, afraid to step back into the circle.

A knot of regret formed in his stomach. He hit the windowsill with his balled fist. "Why in hell did I think coming back here would be easy? Why didn't I just stay away?"

"Excuse me? Did you say something?"

Kat glanced over his shoulder. The receptionist peered around the silk plant. He shook his head. "Sorry. I didn't mean to disturb you. Just thinking out loud."

"Oh." She dismissed him and went back to her computer.

Before he could immerse himself in his musings again, the door marked Private opened and two men came out shaking hands. The older of the two men nodded at the redhead and walked toward the bank of elevators outside the glass wall fronting her desk. The other man stepped back inside the den of privacy and then closed the door.

Turning his attention to the receptionist, Kat waited expectantly.

"You can go in now, Mr.—" she checked the black leather appointment book again, pointedly telling him that she had dismissed him as easily as he had her. Her sultry expression told a different story "—Madison."

In another time, Kat would have made some clever remark, charming forgiveness for his rude behavior from her, but not today. Today, he had more important things on his mind than a redheaded receptionist with welcome in her eyes. Today he thought only of a dark-haired vixen riding away from him, as if wind-devils pursued her...and the things he'd found in his parents' closet sixteen years ago: a small, hand-carved cradle, a metal box holding his adoption papers and a note to the Madisons from a minister outlining how he'd been found.

EMILY FINGERED the tiny key on the chain around her neck. She gazed absently out over the front lawn of her house and pushed at the porch floor with her foot to keep the old rocker in motion.

She'd grown up on Clover Hill Farms. Seen the Kingston fortunes rise with the popularity of their prize stud horses. And she'd seen them fall when a horse died. She'd watched the joining of a stud and mare, then, eleven months later, seen the fruit of that union in the face of a spindly-legged foal. She'd cried when the foals her father had bred for others had left for new homes. And she'd loved it all, every minute of it.

Could she turn her back on it?

The monotonous, back-and-forth motion of the rocker reflected the rhythm of her thoughts.

One minute the idea of caring for a small, helpless human being scared her so much, she actually contemplated, if just for a split second, giving up the farm. The next, the notion of having someone to love and to return her love, to look up to her for guidance, to laugh with her, to share her solitary life, made her go all warm inside.

After an hour of rocking and thinking, she'd come to some pretty startling conclusions. The idea of having the baby and caring for it didn't scare her, or at least not as much as other aspects of this mess. What scared her more was the idea of having to allow a man close enough to accomplish the task. As far as Emily was concerned, she'd rather go nose-to-nose with an unbroken horse than trust a man, any man. There had to be a way…

Her stomach growled, reminding her that she hadn't eaten since the slightly singed toast she'd had for breakfast. The thought of eating another solitary meal made her want to cry. Resolutely, she got up, went inside and grabbed her purse, then headed for her car. Even Tess's prizewinning gray meat loaf was preferable to another sandwich alone—then again, maybe she'd settle for a side trip to her favorite fast-food stop on the way to Honey's for some much needed advice.

EMILY AND HONEY shared the top step on the back porch of Amanda Logan's big, white house. By Bristol standards, the Logan house claimed mansion status. To Em, however, it had always been as warm and welcoming as her own ranch house. She was sure that Honey's mother-in-law had a lot to do with that.

Sipping iced tea and watching Danny chase the yellow balloon she had brought him, Emily mentally snuggled down into the familiar warmth she always felt here.

Honey ran a finger down her sweating glass, leaving behind a trail of water droplets. "So, have you made any decisions about the farm?"

Emily frowned at her sister. "What do you mean decisions about the farm? I'm keeping it, of course. I'll have the baby."

Sitting her glass down at her feet, Honey wiped

her wet hands on her denim-covered thighs, then looked Emily straight in the eye. "How many dates have you had recently?" Emily was about to respond, but Honey held up her hand. "Let me reword that. When was the last time you had a date?"

Snapping her mouth closed, Emily searched her memory. Though she struggled for an answer that would satisfy her sister, none came to mind. The last date she could recall was a year ago on New Year's Eve with Sam Davis, the grandson of one of Rose's friends. Rose said she had arranged the date because Sam was in town for just a few days and his grandmother was concerned that he'd be alone New Year's Eve, but Emily wasn't sure Rose hadn't had an ulterior motive. If she had, it hadn't worked. Sam was nice, but certainly didn't rock the earth beneath Emily's feet.

Honey leaned back, a knowing look filling her eyes. "I thought so. You haven't had a date in so long, you can't even recall when it was."

"I can too recall it."

"When?"

"Last New Year's Eve."

Honey's red lips quirked to one side. "That was arranged. It doesn't count. Besides, Em, that's over a year ago."

Avoiding her sister's censuring look, Emily watched Danny chase his balloon across the lawn, hit it, then bound off after it again. She felt a bit like the balloon. In the past two days, she'd been battered from pillar to post with other people's conclusions about her life. She needed to come to some decisions, something that would signal she'd taken back control. But Honey usually thought in absolutes and Emily had none, so she couldn't broach the subject just yet.

Grabbing for something to steer the conversation in a new direction, she settled on one of the other unexpected events of her long day. "Guess who's back in town."

Casting Emily an I-know-you're-avoiding-me look, Honey asked, "Who?"

"Kat."

Sitting up straight, Honey gaped at Emily. "Kat Madison?"

"One and the same."

"What's he doing back here?"

"I saw him working on the old Madison place."

"Do you think he's back to stay?"

Denying the hope that surged through her at that consideration, Emily shook her head. "No. I have the feeling he's fixing it up to sell it, then leaving again." The thought sat in her stomach like a large rock.

"And?"

Emily stared at her sister. "And what?"

"What happened?"

"Nothing. What did you expect to happen? I haven't seen the man in sixteen years." She threw Honey an impatient look and turned her attention back to Danny. Uncomfortable with having to relate to Honey what she'd said to Kat, Emily switched subjects for the second time. "So, what do you think I should do about conceiving a baby?"

A heavy sigh came from Honey's side of the porch step. "As I see it, as long as you're determined to go this route, you have three choices—adoption, in vitro fertilization, or the good old-fashioned way."

Standing, Emily walked to the white, lacy porch railing and balanced herself atop it, keeping her balance by hooking one sneakered toe in the cutout of the vertical boards. "Adoption takes forever. I don't have forever. And the old-fashioned way is not even a consideration."

"Why?"

Not believing the feigned look of innocence on Honey's face, Emily frowned. "Because that entails a relationship with a man, and, if you recall, we just established that my social life is nil. Besides I always felt sex was highly overrated."

"Hells bells, Em, your first experience was with Joey Sloan. He didn't know what the zipper on the front of his pants was for until he was twelve. What can you expect? I never did understand what you saw in him."

"He liked horses."

Honey snorted, then glanced at her son racing after his balloon. "Sex doesn't have to be like that. When it's the right time with the right person, it's…"

"It's what?"

Honey turned to her, as if waking from a dream.

"Let me make this simple for you. It's *not* Joey Sloan in the back seat of his father's old sedan parked on the overlook above the village dump."

Emily glowered at her sister, then tapped her cheek with the tip of her blunt nail, not wishing to get any deeper into the subject of her teenage male preferences. Besides, Honey didn't need to know that an emotional relationship or the possibility of one had no part in Emily's plan for her future. "Artificial insemination has its possibilities, however."

"Good grief, Emily, you sound like you're talking about one of your horses."

"The problem is—" Emily went on, as if Honey hadn't said a word "—I'd have to find a donor."

Honey emitted a very unladylike snort. "Why don't you just stroll down Main Street stopping every man you see until you find one willing to donate a few of his little guys to the cause."

Emily threw her sister a disparaging look. "Can we be serious here for a minute? We're talking about a baby for goodness' sake." She shook her head. "I don't want just any man fathering my child. I want to know who he is."

"Why?"

"Because I want my child to have the best possible start in life that he can."

A smile curved Honey's lips.

"What's that grin for?"

"I was just thinking that the idea of this baby has really got you interested and not just because you can keep the farm. You want this baby, don't you?"

Avoiding her sister's gaze, Emily gave a non-committal shrug. "Maybe."

For a long time, neither of them said anything, each lost in their thoughts. Emily once again pictured herself with a baby, soft, tiny, warm and loving. Although the picture left her smiling inside, the responsibility still scared her half to death.

Honey sat up straight and turned to Emily, her eyes glowing, her lips curved in a self-satisfied smile. "I've got it. If you're so determined to do this, why not ask Kat?"

At that precise moment, Danny's balloon popped, and so did Emily's daydreams about the baby. When her heart had stopped doing doubletime, Emily turned to her sister.

"Kat?"

A knowing expression transformed Honey's face. "I always felt you and he had something going as kids. And who was it who always rode to your rescue—" Honey went silent. She stared at Emily.

Emily swirled the suggestion around in her mind. Even as angry as she was at Kat, the suggestion appealed to her in a very comforting way.

"Em, I was kidding. You're not seriously considering—"

She left her perch on the railing and came back to hunker down next to Honey on the step. The last thing she wanted was the baby's father hanging around. With Kat's nomadic track record, he was quickly becoming a strong candidate for fatherhood. "Why not?"

"Emily Kingston...." Honey grabbed her sister's arm. "Are you nuts? You have no idea what he's been doing since you last saw him."

"But he's perfect. Clean-cut. Good-looking. He's a rolling stone, never settles down. He'd probably donate his sperm, finish the house and hit the road again. Voilà! No attachments."

Honey thought for a minute. "Healthy. Is he healthy?"

"A doctor's exam will determine that. I'm sure you can't donate sperm if you aren't healthy and I'm sure they must do some kind of tests, even if you know who the donor is." Emily waited, knowing by the look on her face that Honey had not given up. She didn't have to wait long.

"Okay. What about willing? You don't know that he'd even do this." She smiled as if in victory. "I wouldn't start buying the layette just yet."

For a second Emily was stumped, then she recalled a trump card Honey hadn't counted on. "He owes me after walking out on me without explanation. Maybe, if he does this for me, I might forgive him."

Honey shook her arm. "Em, you're letting your desire to keep the farm do your thinking. For all you know, Kat could be an escaped convict, a serial killer, an alien." Emily cast her a look of incredulity. "Okay, so the alien thingy was a bit much. What I'm trying to say is that this is not a good idea. Besides, how do you plan on explaining this to Rose?"

"I"ll figure out something. She won't be home for weeks. I have plenty of time. And as far as asking Kat goes, I disagree. With a few ground rules—" She jumped up. "I have to go home and figure out how to contact him."

She kissed her sister's cheek, then raced down the stairs to her truck, yelling goodbye to Danny as she climbed into the driver's seat. In the rearview mirror, she could see Honey standing on the porch, mouth agape, hands outstretched, as if wondering what just happened. For once, she'd left her older sister speechless.

Emily didn't have to wonder what had just happened. She'd had an epiphany. Kat had always helped her before. Why not this time? All she wanted was one healthy, enthusiastic sperm to conceive her baby. Surely he could spare one. Besides, he owed her for running out on her.

KAT SETTLED into the black leather chair across from J. R. Pritchard. Pritchard looked more like a successful CEO than a P.I. Navy suit, burgundy-and-beige tie executed in a perfect Windsor knot beneath the button-down collar of a crisp, white shirt. Definitely not the Bogart type Kat had anticipated.

"Mr. Madison—"

"Kat."

Pritchard raised an eyebrow. "Kat. What can I do for you?"

Reaching into his back pocket, Kat extracted a worn, brown leather wallet. From it, he pulled a slip of paper, which he unfolded, then passed to Pritchard. "This is a rubbing off the end of a handmade cradle. I want to know who made the cradle and who it was made for."

Pritchard studied the design, one Kat was very familiar with: a hand-carved, crude reproduction of a rose twined around an equally crude heart, all enclosed in a circle.

"I've never seen anything like this before." Pritchard continued to study the rubbing. "There's a good chance that someone might recognize it for that very reason. There's also a good chance, again for that very reason, that you'll never find out who carved it." He tossed the paper on his desk. "Why is it important that you find the artist? Is this cradle an antique or something?"

An explanation hung on Kat's lips. No one knew about the cradle or his adoption. He didn't like sharing that knowledge. "The rubbing might have something to do with my birth parents. I was adopted by Hilda and Charles Madison when I was ten months old." He pulled another folded sheet of paper from his wallet. This one showed the wear marks of having been unfolded many times. He handed it to Pritchard.

He nodded, then looked at the paper. "Ah, so you're looking to be reunited with your birth parents."

"No." Kat's tone was much sterner than he'd planned. Pritchard's head jerked up. "No emotional reunions. Just find the artist and the information I asked for, then call me. I'll take it from there.'' All Kat wanted to know was why anyone would abandon a ten-month-old infant to strangers and walk away. He didn't need Pritchard digging around in his life—not that he had anything to hide. But some things were better off staying between a man and his conscience.

Pritchard stared at him for a long time, then shrugged, as if he really didn't care to know Kat's reasoning and that suited Kat just fine. He had no intention of sharing it. "Any hurry on this?"

Kat shook his head. "None." He'd already spent sixteen years searching, he could wait a while longer.

It HAD BEEN a full two days since Emily had talked to Honey, her decision to ask Kat to father her child already taking form in her mind. Trouble was, when she got home, her nerve had deserted her. After the things she'd said to him, how could she now ask for such a monumental favor?

She leaned against the rail fence separating the corrals. She still hadn't forgiven him for deserting her all those years ago, but that was something she'd have to worry about later. Right now, she didn't have time to waste. She needed a father for her child. Correction. She needed Kat to father her child.

The ring of a hammer pounding nails into wood echoed across the west pasture. Her fingers unconsciously sought and curled around the tiny key lying against her collarbone. The smooth metal, warmed by her body heat, and its familiar shape gave her courage. After doing one last mental check of her list of stipulations, she swallowed hard and headed toward Kat's house.

Plan A was officially in motion.

Chapter Three

Kat laid the pry bar aside, pulled a soiled rag from his back pocket, then wiped the perspiration from his face and upper torso. Standing back a few paces, he gazed at his former home. He nodded to himself in satisfaction, then smiled.

He'd been very careful about his plans for renovating the old Victorian house. The last thing he wanted to do was remove the things that gave it character, and, he had to admit, the familiarity he cherished. Thankfully, only the corner where the living room had been would have to be rebuilt. The rest of the house had survived. He had only a few more boards to pull off, then he'd check the studs for fire damage. By next week, he could start to rebuild. If all went well, he'd have the house ready to go on the market in about four weeks.

A noise behind him drew his attention from the house. He swung around. Emily stood just inside the line of trees dividing their land, a blanket folded over her arm and a picnic hamper at her feet. Sunlight danced off her rich brown hair, which was caught back in a long braid. Her face, devoid of all makeup, creased in a tentative smile that tore at his insides. Her curves, encased by jeans and a bright yellow sweater, reminded him again that Emily had become a woman. Something inside him mourned missing the transformation from the little girl with the dirty face and the ripped jeans into this breathtaking beauty.

What had brought her here? After their last encounter, he'd thought she would avoid him at all costs. As she walked past him to the base of the large oak hanging over most of the yard, the smell of perfume drifted to him. Emily? Perfume? She'd never smelled like anything but the horses she loved.

"Hi." She set the basket down, then spread the blanket in the shade.

"Hi, yourself."

"I thought you might want some lunch." She pointed at the picnic basket, the same one they'd hauled on many picnics as kids. Then she half-smiled. "Actually, it's kind of a peace offering."

Why did she feel compelled to come with a peace offering, when he was the one who should be apologizing? Tempted to lighten the moment by chiding her about her cooking, he held back. With the ease of their past association gone and the tension that hung between them, he didn't feel comfortable teasing her anymore. Instead, he offered a weak, "Great! My stomach was beginning to think my throat had been cut."

Avoiding his gaze, Emily opened the basket.

"Rose is away, so I had to make the sandwiches."

"Rose?"

"My housekeeper. She came here after…well, after." Fumbling with the contents of the basket, she looked at him expectantly. "I made—"

"—peanut butter and banana sandwiches," Kat finished for her.

She brightened, as if pleased that he remembered her favorite sandwich. He smiled back. Her expression became hesitant, as if his smile made her uneasy. She quickly turned away. "Cooking was never my strong suit." She fussed with laying out the contents of the basket, then glanced at the house. "What are you going to do with it when you get it done?"

"Sell it." He noted the stiffness in her body begin to drain away. Relief that he wouldn't be right on her doorstep? Her next words answered his question.

"Then you're not planning on living here?"

Was that a note of hope in her voice? "No." An honest answer, if a bit evasive; he didn't plan to live in the house. Again, Kat thought he saw relief in her posture. The intense surge of disappointment he experienced took him by surprise.

The air between them became thick enough to ride a horse over. Kat searched for words, any words. Anything was better than this tension. Anything to bridge this gulf separating them. He sighed. Only one thing would do that and he had to be the one to do it.

"Emily, I'm sorry that I took off and never said anything to you."

She turned slowly toward him.

"It was unfair. I wish I could tell you why I did it, but I can't. Not yet." He took her hand. "I promise that someday I will, but not right now. Trust me, okay?" Her fingers tightened around his. That small gesture brought something alive inside him that had been cold and dead. "I want to be friends again. Is that possible?"

Even as he said the words, currents of awareness raced up his arm from their clenched hands. For the first time in his life, Kat wasn't sure exactly what he felt for Emily. Was it just friendship?

Before he could decide, she removed her hand from his. "I don't know. Can we?"

The pain of Kat's leaving still sat heavy on Emily's heart. She wanted to know why he'd gone, but he obviously wasn't going to tell her.

He'd promised long ago that he'd always be there for her, and he hadn't been. It didn't take a genius to figure out that Kat's promises were about as substantial as her father's. She'd trusted him when they were kids. Dare she trust him again?

"I'd like us to be friends, Squirt."

She looked into his dark eyes for a long time, trying to assess his sincerity. He winked. That familiar gesture, coupled with the use of the nickname he'd given her years ago, gave birth to a warm rush of contentment inside her. She'd missed Kat, but she truly hadn't realized just how much until she'd come face-to-face with the one person who'd made her childhood tolerable. She wanted him in her life, but not just for the sake of fathering her child. She wanted her friend back, even if she wasn't sure she could ever trust him again.

KAT SIGHED, laid aside the core of the apple he'd just devoured for desert and then leaned back against the old oak. Shadows covered his face.

"Squirt—" He studied her, then brushed at a stray strand of hair the slight breeze had deposited on her cheek. "I guess I'd better find a new name for you. You went and grew up on me."

Emily wanted to remind him that, if he'd stayed around, he'd have been here for her growing-up, but she was too busy fighting the tingles of awareness racing the length of her body. She abruptly leaned away, breaking contact with his fingers.

What was wrong with her?

This was Kat, her buddy, not some hunk trying to seduce her. Resisting the urge to touch her cheek, she pushed the feelings aside. She had to concentrate on wording what she'd come here to ask him.

"Oh, oh. I remember that look. What's going on in that devious little mind of yours?" He leaned down to see her face. "What do you want me to jump off this time?"

She shook her head, trying to produce a wide-eyed look of innocence.

Kat sat up, then leaned toward her. "Nope. That look hasn't washed with me since you were six, and I took the blame for you almost burning up the field while you were practicing your Girl Scout campfire skills. You're forgetting I know you too well. I haven't forgotten that your teeth nibbling on your bottom lip means you're up to something.'' He smiled, then gently pried her lip free. ''Out with it.''

It annoyed her that she hadn't been aware, until he'd pointed it out, that she'd been gnawing on her lip or that she'd slipped so easily into their familiar ways. And it annoyed her even more that his casual touch had started those tingles up again.

Concentrate, Emily.

He'd given her the perfect opening. Instead of worrying about some crazy hormonal reaction, she needed to be thinking about how to form the words to get his agreement. After all, it wasn't every day that she asked a man to father a child for her.

''I'm going to have a baby.'' The words tumbled past her lips before she could stop them. Cautiously, she glanced at Kat.

His skin had paled slightly. He pushed himself to his feet. His mouth hardened. ''What do you want me to say? Good going, Em?''

The bite in his words surprised her. What was he getting his shorts in a knot about? Then it hit her. He thought she meant she was pregnant already.

Before she could rectify her blunder, he turned away from her. ''And who's the lucky man?''

The edge in his voice cut through her confidence. She lowered her gaze. ''You.'' When he didn't reply right away, she glanced up.

Kat had swung around, his eyes wide, his mouth hanging agape. ''Excuse me? Would you remind repeating that?''

''I said, you.'' *Oh damn! None of this is going the way I planned.* Emily stood, then hurried to him, trying to ignore how the noon sun kissed his bronze skin. She had to stop this stupid preoccupation with the man Kat had become and keep her mind centered on business. "I'm not pregnant already. I need to *get* pregnant. Kat, I *need* to have a baby, and I want you to be its father." She touched his forearm, but he moved away.

His obvious confusion brought his thick dark brows together in a frown. "What the hell are you talking about?"

Impatient with herself and fumbling for the right words, Emily stamped her foot. "If you'll sit down and stop roaming around like a grazing horse, I'll tell you."

Glaring at her, Kat flopped down at the base of the tree, then ran his hands through his hair. Resting his forearm across his bent knee, he waited. "Start talking and try to make it understandable this time."

Emily retook her seat on the blanket. She tucked one leg beneath the other, then raised her chin to face him. She cleared her throat. "Lawrence Tippens called me to his office a few days ago. He said he'd found a codicil to my father's will."

Sitting a little straighter as Emily related what Lawrence had told her, Kat listened intently. She explained why adoption or any of the other options wouldn't do. Then she waited while he digested the information.

He couldn't believe his ears. Frank Kingston had done some pretty outrageous things, but where did he get off blackmailing his own daughter into having a child? "I take it you're going to do it."

She nodded. "There was never any question about it."

"And exactly how do I figure into this?"

"I want you to donate your...sperm and father the baby."

He laughed, but stopped abruptly when he saw her frown. "You're serious aren't you?" He had to be dreaming.

She scowled at him. "If I wasn't serious, do you think we'd be having this conversation? I don't make it a habit of popping out babies just for ha-has."

"No, I mean about me donating my sperm. Why was I chosen to be the lucky one?"

She shrugged. "We've known each other forever. You know how much the farm means to me. You must know I'd never ask this if I could find another way to keep the farm."

Suddenly aware of an unfounded anger rising in him, Kat fought to keep it tamped down. "So you're bringing a small life into this world just to save your farm?"

Emily jumped to her feet and stood over him, her face flaming red, her fists jammed on her hips. "Are you crazy? Do you think I'd do that to any child? I want this baby for me. I'd want it even if I'd never had the farm." She waved her hand. "I'll admit, I didn't want it at first. After all, it did come as somewhat of a shock. It still scares the hell out of me. But I've had time to think and I really want the baby, Kat—for myself." Her face softened. "Really."

Maybe he was nuts, but he believed her. "Okay. Sit down and cool your heels." He waited while she resumed her seat. "Have you given any consideration to doing this the way most people do? You know, love, marriage, bed, two people...." He had no reason to finish the sentence. The blush that rose to her cheeks told him she'd gotten his drift.

"That's out of the question. The last thing I'm looking for is emotional involvement." She pulled a piece of paper from her jeans. "I wrote down the conditions." She unfolded it and began ticking off the things she'd listed. "You'll need a complete physical. When the doctor says you're healthy, you'll donate the sperm, then I'll be inseminated and you can go your merry way. No attachments, not complications, no responsibilities, no—"

Kat jumped to his feet, his anger boiling to the surface and out of his control, not that he even tried to control it. "Let me get this straight. You want me to agree to my child being the end result of an hour in a locked bathroom with a paper cup and a girly magazine? Then I'm supposed to walk away as if the child didn't exist?"

"That's putting it a little crudely, but essentially, yes, that's right."

He raked his hands through his hair in an effort to keep from shaking her senseless. Gazing out over the meadows, stretching beyond the back of the house and dotted with grazing horses, he closed his eyes and saw a small wooden cradle holding a tiny baby and sitting on a stranger's doorstep.

"No."

"No?" She scrambled to her feet. "You mean, no, you won't do it?"

He swung on her. "You got it, Em."

"But you've always helped me out when I needed you. Why not now? I won't make any demands on you as the father. I promise. You'll be free to leave."

She just didn't get it. He *wanted* demands made on him. He *wanted* to take part in the life of any child that carried his blood and his genes. He would not do to a child what had been done to him. But he couldn't tell her that without telling her everything, and he wasn't ready to share any of that until he got the answer he craved.

"We're not kids anymore, Em. You're not planning to swipe apples from Old Man Watkins' orchard. I'm not going to blindly follow your lead this time. This is too damned important."

"Don't you think I know that? I'm not asking that you blindly follow my lead. I've told you everything I expect of you. All you have to do is agree to the terms."

"And after the baby's born. I just walk away, right?"

"Free to forget us."

He ran his fingers through his wind-rumpled hair. "Em, I'd jump out of a tree again for you, with or without a parachute, but this time I think it's going to hurt too much when I land. You need to find yourself another guinea pig." He stepped to her side. "I may be an oddball, but by damn, no kid of mine will be." Skirting around her, he stalked toward the house, grabbed the pry bar, then began tearing at a burned board.

A vehicle turned into the driveway. Ignoring the new arrival, Kat glanced over his shoulder in time to catch the flash of Emily's yellow sweater disappearing into the trees. The remains of their picnic lay scattered over the blanket at the base of the tree.

His heart hurt for Emily and himself. Didn't she know that he'd gladly give her anything she asked? Anything—except the right to raise his child without him?

The door on the newly arrived vehicle slammed. Kat turned toward the sound, his heart still heavy about the conversation he'd just finished with Emily. Dave Thornton strode toward him.

"Hi. I was out this way to attend a meeting and thought I'd drop by to see what kind of progress you're making."

Throwing down the pry bar and glancing once more toward where Em had disappeared into the trees, Kat turned to his visitor. "I'm doing okay. Right on schedule."

"Schedule?"

"I'd like to put the house on the market in a month." He shrugged. "It's not written in stone, but it gives me a target." He gestured toward two saw horses. "Have a seat." Once Dave was settled, Kat searched for something to take his mind off Emily's proposition. "You say you're out here for a meeting?"

"Yeah. The Horseman's Benevolent Association." He flushed. "I'm president this year. I don't need the extra work, but it's a good cause. We're knee-deep in planning our annual charity drive." Dave grinned. "I don't suppose I could talk you into donating the house when it's done?"

"No. The only charity that's gonna see the money from this house is Kat Madison."

"Too bad. It's a nice house in a prime location." He pulled a business card from his jacket pocket. "I'm a real estate broker, too." He grinned sheepishly. "Hey, with a kid on the way and two more at home, every little bit helps." He handed Kat the card. "When it's ready, give me a call. I'd be happy to show it for you."

Kat took the card, then walked Dave to his car, but he was barely aware of him pulling out of the driveway.

Kat's attention was on the line of trees. Here he was talking about selling his home, and Em was fighting to keep hers. And he'd refused to help her. He felt like a louse.

SINCE EM and Dave had left, Kat had got nothing done. His mind was everywhere on everything but his work. Anger at Emily and her harebrained proposition still churned in his gut.

Methodically, as if compartmentalizing his thoughts also, he began gathering his tools and placing them precisely in the toolbox. The exercise served to cool his anger enough to be able to think rationally.

Once he got past the anger, the idea of having a baby with Em wasn't at all unappealing. He thought about her tight jeans, her sweater clinging to her endless curves, her sweet kissable mouth, about—

Yes, the more he thought about it, the more appealing it became. The one aspect that stopped him, however, was leaving after the baby was conceived. Deserting his duties as a father to his own child? Missing out on its life? How could she even ask such a thing of him?

He wondered just how much Em wanted this baby. Was she just looking for a way to keep her home? He recalled her passionate words and the pleading look on her face.

I really want the baby, Kat—for myself. Really.

Not a doubt remained in his mind that she did want the baby. By why, if not for legal reasons? Could Em just be so in need of love that she felt a baby would fill the hole in her life?

The answers eluded him. But of one thing he was sure. Em needed him. He could help her. The rest would have to sort itself out. Besides, he'd be living right here, so she'd have to let him see his child. Wouldn't she?

He threw the last of the tools in the box, snapped the lid closed, then hefted it into the back of his truck. He rinsed off in a bucket of water, then grabbed his shirt off the porch railing. He slid his arms into the sleeves and left the front open. As he walked past the oak tree, he glanced down at the remains of their lunch. Good excuse as any to show up on her doorstep.

As EMILY entered the house through the kitchen door, the phone rang. She hurried to pick it up.

"Hello."

"Hello, sweetheart."

"Rose! Hi!" After the episode with Kat, Emily really needed the sound of a comforting voice. "Where are you?"

"Still in Mexico. I just wanted to see how you're doing."

Emily wasn't about to go into long-distance details of what was going on in her life. Time enough for that when Rose came home. Besides, Emily needed time to figure out how to tell Rose what was going on.

As if Rose could see it, she smiled. "I'm fine. What about you? When are you going to stop this globe-trotting and come home?"

A high-pitched laugh filled the phone. "We're in Mexico City. Right on schedule. We won't be home for another two weeks. Although, if Carol and I had our way, we'd put Helen on the next flight to Albany."

"Oh? Something wrong?" Last time Emily had spoken to Rose, her two traveling companions were fine.

"Nothing that being in the good ol' US of A wouldn't cure. Helen drank some of the water down here and she's been feeling a little peaked for the last couple of days, if you know what I mean."

Emily knew. She'd heard horror stories about what happened when you drank the water in foreign countries.

"Carol and I have been trying to get her to go home. She's got her back up and flatly refuses."

Standing straighter with concern for her housekeeper's elderly friend, Emily frowned. "Is she going to be okay? Maybe you should just stick her on the next flight home."

Again Rose laughed. "She'd kick and scream all the way to the airport. She's determined to stick it out. Says she saved for ten years for this vacation, and she's gonna make the most of it, even if it's from the inside of a bathroom." A door closed in the background. "Gotta go. Carol just came back with lunch. You take care and I'll see you in a couple of weeks."

"I miss you," she said impulsively, then quickly added, "I love you."

"Love you more," came Rose's familiar reply, then silence. "You sure you're doing okay?"

Emily must have given away something of her mood in her tone of voice. Deliberately, she brightened it. "Of course, I'm fine. Honey comes over every other day and checks to make sure I don't starve to death. Don't worry about me. I'll survive. You enjoy your vacation."

"All right. If you say so. Bye, sweetheart."

"Bye."

She returned the receiver to the wall phone and leaned her head against the cool plastic. How she missed Rose, and not just for her cooking. She needed someone to help her through this mess, if only emotionally. Rose always managed to get Emily's feet planted firmly on solid ground. Right now, she felt as if she were being sucked up in the middle of a tornado.

Resolutely, knowing that self-pity would get her nowhere, Emily pushed herself upright and turned toward the sink. In the doorway, outlined by the sun, stood Kat. She couldn't see his face. But she knew. The half-gainer her insides did confirmed it.

Unsure of what to say, she said nothing.

He held out the blanket and picnic hamper. "You forgot these."

"Thanks." She took them and placed them on one of the kitchen chairs. Another silence stretched out.

"Em—"

"Kat—"

He smiled. "You first."

"No, you first."

"I've been thinking about what you asked me to do, and I've changed my mind."

Emily's insides did a flip. She wasn't sure if relief caused it or that there was a very good chance she would soon become a mother. "You'll father my baby?"

He nodded. "But we do it my way, on my terms, or not at all." Kat came the rest of the way into the kitchen, then sat on the edge of the table. He looked directly at Emily.

She sobered. "I'm listening."

"First of all, we'll get married."

Chapter Four

"Married!" Emily sank into the chair behind her and stared openmouthed across the kitchen table at Kat. Had he lost his mind, or she her hearing? "You did say *married?*"

"Yes. Married, as in old shoes, rice, orange blossoms." Although his tone was light, his eyes held a seriousness that disturbed Emily. "As in a legitimate mother and father for *our* child."

She didn't like the emphasis he put on *our,* but her senses hadn't recovered enough to retaliate. Besides, deep down, it warmed her that he cared enough for their yet-to-be-conceived child that he wanted it never to have to face life without the legitimacy of its parents' marriage attached to its name.

"Why don't you make some coffee and we'll discuss the rest of the conditions?"

The rest? Wasn't marriage enough? How many more outrageous demands was he going to hit her between the eyes with?

Kat jumped suddenly to his feet. "Never mind. I

remember your coffee. I'll make it." He went to the cabinet, then search for and found the coffee canister. Methodically, he went through the ritual of brewing a full pot of coffee.

While he worked, Emily watched him, carefully assessing what she saw. Kat had become downright disgustingly gorgeous. With her own dark-brown hair trapped somewhere between chestnut and sable, she'd always envied the way his wavy hair glowed with the bluish highlights that only true ebony hair has. His shoulders, broadened and muscled from hard work, strained at the seams of the worn, blue cotton workshirt, as did the corded muscles of his legs against his faded denim jeans, as if his entire body would have been more comfortable without the encumbrance of clothes.

Whoa! She stopped that train of thought dead in its tracks.

Looking beyond the outer trappings that come with time and age, she sought the man. And he was there, in all his tantalizing glory. Kat no longer resembled the uncertain, gangly boy with too much arm and leg to control gracefully, the boy she remembered. Now, he moved with the confidence of a man who knew what he wanted, asked no one's pardon, and as a result, savored life to its fullest.

She admired his confidence. Entering into marriage with Kat took on a less threatening aura. Why, she wasn't certain, but at least the prospect no longer had the power to paralyze her vocal chords.

"I suppose marriage would certainly make it a lot easier to explain why you're suddenly living with me. And after the baby is conceived, it would be simple to get an annulment.'' She laughed lightly. ''I mean, it's not as if we'd be sleeping together or anything like that. So there wouldn't be the physical thing to overcome, right?''

Kat's movements stopped abruptly. A warning signal shot through her insides.

''Right, Kat?''

He stood statue-still, then, keeping his back to her, he punched the start button on the coffeemaker.

''Kat, answer me.''

Panic flooded through her. He couldn't ask that of her. She couldn't sleep with him. Not Kat. Not the man who had been her playmate. The man who had bandaged her skinned knees. *The man whose touch had, that very afternoon, sent tingles cascading through her entire body.*

She stared at his stiff back waiting for an answer. The coffeemaker belched and gurgled. Seconds later, the aroma of brewing coffee filled the kitchen, a smell she normally loved, but one that now threatened to turn her nervous stomach with its richness.

''Kat?''

Gripping the edge of the sink with his fingers, Kat prepared to face Emily with the one demand he wasn't at all sure she would go for. He swung slowly to face her, then leaned against the sink with a nonchalance he was far from feeling. Why was he so uptight? It was her future on the line, not his. If she said no, then she would be the loser, not him.

''I'm afraid we *will* be sharing a bed. I won't

agree unless the baby is conceived the old-fashioned way.'' There—it was out.

''Oh no!'' Emily rose from the chair, shaking her head adamantly. ''No! Absolutely not.'' She looked at him, her eyes reflecting her distressed state.

Kat looked away. He knew how easily he could succumb to Emily's pain. Wasn't the fact that he was standing here making this proposal proof of that? ''We do it that way, Em, or not at all.''

She glanced around the kitchen. ''I can't...I don't think...I...we...'' She paused and faced him squarely. ''How could you ask this of me?''

He turned back to her. ''How could you ask that a child be conceived any other way?''

''But why?''

He hesitated, not wanting to tell her how the idea of sharing Emily's bed had become a very appealing prospect. That he was feeling things for her that made no sense, things a man shouldn't feel for a female he called his friend. But that was his problem and right now, he had to make Emily see that his way was best for the child.

''Think about it, Em. When the child grows up and starts asking you questions about his birth, what are you going to tell him? That his dad went into the doctor's examination room and—''

''No! Of course not.''

''Then what?''

''I don't know. I hadn't though that far ahead.'' Emily sank back into the chair.

''As I recall, you rarely do.'' She glared at him. Kat crossed the floor and sat next to her, then took her hands. He caressed the ridge of her knuckles with the slow movement of his thumb. "You must see this is best for the baby." Emily remained still. Her fingers twitched in his, as if her nerves were going haywire.

He hastened to ease her apprehension. "I would never force you into anything you didn't want to do." He stared deep into her eyes. "You do know that, don't you?" She nodded. "We can get married and, keeping in mind the time limitations, when you feel comfortable taking the next step, that's when we'll do it and not a moment sooner."

Emily listened, trying to ignore those tingles starting to erupt under the caress of his calloused thumb. His rough skin brought to mind the grit of sandpaper and at the same time, the sensual caress of silk. Whatever he'd been doing for sixteen years, it hadn't been sitting behind a desk, pushing papers. She marshaled her veering thoughts back to the conversation.

His assurance that they'd do this at her pace put her mind somewhat at ease. And, he was offering her the opportunity to keep her home and have the baby she wanted so much. So, why was she hesitating?

Think, Emily. This isn't all that hard to answer. Something is happening here. You're terrified of sharing his bed. You're afraid you can't do it and remain detached. In fact, you're damned sure you can't.

Considering her strange reactions from just having Kat look at her, casually touch her…. Just the memory sent her emotions darting about like a crazed paper airplane and her senses spinning like an out-of-control top. Having him around all the time, especially in her bed, could be far too dangerous.

What in heaven's name had come over her? She certainly had no attachment to Kat beyond friendship, but she was smart enough, honest enough and woman enough to admit that what she was feeling could easily escalate into something far more serious. Something she might not be able to control. Something they both would regret.

Time was running out and she had nowhere else to turn. But he'd said nothing about leaving after the baby was conceived. She reminded herself that when he finished fixing the old house, he'd sell it and probably move on.

If she agreed to his proposal—and right now she saw no way she couldn't—she'd worry about permanently removing him from her life after the baby was conceived. In the meantime, despite the intimate association they'd have to have to accomplish that, she'd keep an emotional distance between them. She could do it. She *had* to do it.

"Well, Em? What's it gonna be?"

"Okay. We'll do it your way. You'll need to move in before Rose—" She stopped abruptly and jumped from the chair to begin pacing the kitchen. "Rose! Good grief, I forgot all about her."

"Who's Rose?"

"I told you, she's my housekeeper. She's been with me ever since Mom died." She glanced at

Kat's questioning expression. "About a month after you left." She resumed pacing. "I'll have to explain this to her. I can't tell her that we're only pretending to be happily married."

"Why tell her anything?"

Emily stopped pacing and stared at him. "When she left, I was single, without a steady boyfriend, much less aspirations of marriage and having a child. When she comes home, she'll find a man I'm calling my husband living here. Offhand, I'd say I could bank on her asking a few questions." Not to mention how hurt she'd be that Emily hadn't waited for her to come home before having the wedding.

"So, we met and fell in love after she left. It was a whirlwind courtship." He grinned. "We were once playmates and when I came back, we realized that we were in love. Simple."

Emily's stomach flipped. She really wished he'd stop smiling and touching and all the other things he did that turned her mind to mush.

She hated lying to Rose, but she couldn't see any other way around telling her sharp-eyed, motherly housekeeper that they were married and making a baby so she could keep the farm. Inside, she grimaced at the sound of that. This had gone beyond the farm to a much more personal goal. She wanted this baby. She had to start thinking in terms of this precious little life she'd soon be holding and loving.

"I guess that's the only way out. When you leave, after the baby is conceived, then I'll just tell everyone we mistook friendship for love and realized we'd made a terrible mistake."

Kat looked uncomfortable. He came to her, then took her hands in his. "There's one thing more."

Not about to have to contend with those tingles again, she removed her hand from his and took a step back. Emily held her breath. How much worse could it be?

"I want full visitation rights with the child."

"That wasn't part of the conditions."

"It wasn't part of *your* conditions, but it's a part of *mine*." Kat waited. As far as he was concerned, this was the one most important condition. If she wouldn't agree to this one, then she could scrap the rest. "Well?"

"You know you have me backed into a corner, don't you?"

He smiled. "As I recall, I used to be the one left with no escape from your schemes. This time the tables are turned, Emily Kingston. Take it or leave it."

The jaws of his proposition closed on her. She took a deep breath, but quickly exhaled when his masculine scent drowned out the aroma of the brewing coffee and her head began to whirl. "All right. We'll figure something out on visitations later."

If he was like some men, as soon as the newness of fatherhood wore thin, visitations would be the least of her worries. But, deep inside, something told her Kat couldn't be measured by the same yardstick as other men. He was a man unto himself.

He walked to the back door. His hand on the knob, he turned. "One more thing."

"What now? You want my oath in blood?"

He flashed that heart-stopping smile. "A thought, but no. You always could be counted on to keep your word. I see no reason to doubt it now." His expression became dead serious. "I promise, no matter what happens, everything will work out." Then he opened the door and stepped onto the porch, closing the door behind him.

Emily stared at the closed portal for a long time. Sixteen years ago Kat had promised her he'd always be there for her. Then he'd disappeared. What had become of that promise when her mother died, then her father and she'd been faced with running this place alone? What had become of Kat Madison's promises when loneliness ate at her like a hungry rodent and she'd desperately needed her friend to talk to?

She might have to depend on him to become a mother, but she didn't have to count on his promises, and she wouldn't. Long ago, she'd learned a man's promise was about as substantial as smoke.

KAT SAT behind the wheel of his truck in Emily's driveway for a long time. Staring at the two-story white ranch house, he allowed the events of the last hour to play through his mind. When he got as far as Emily realizing they'd be sharing a bed, he stopped.

The more thought he gave to that eventuality, the more he found himself drawn to the prospect. However, Emily wanted to keep things impersonal. Impersonal. How could he share a bed with Emily and keep it impersonal? Did she think he was made of stone? And he was about certain that Ms. Kingston wouldn't be able to accomplish such a feat either. He'd noticed how she squirmed under his gaze and how she avoided physical contact, how her mind seemed to wander when he held her hand.

Kat smiled. Okay, Emily, you want impersonal, that's just what you'll get. Even if it kills us both. Anything beyond that will be your call.

Anyway, he wasn't at all sure his plans for staying in Bristol would work out. But with a child and Emily in the offing, he would do his damndest to put down roots for the first time in sixteen years.

He slapped the steering wheel to punctuate his decision, then turned the key and started the engine. As he swung the truck around to leave, he glanced at the house and smiled when he saw Emily peeking from behind a curtain.

He grinned. "Impersonal, huh?"

"I CAN'T BELIEVE you're actually going through with this." Honey stared across the bill-strewn dining-room table at Emily. "And I find it even harder to believe that Kat actually agreed."

"Why do you find that so hard to believe?" Actually, Emily was still reeling herself from Kat's fairly fast decision to go along with her.

"The man is either desperate for a woman or absolutely nuts. I haven't figured out which yet."

Emily smoothed her hand over the silky, polished mahogany table that Honey often used as her desk so she could keep an eye on Danny as he played outside. "Since this was your idea, I'd have thought you'd be pleased."

"It was a joke, little sister. But you do what you have to. Why *he's* agreeing to do this, still worries me."

Resisting the urge to defend Kat's compliance, even to Honey, Emily steered the conversation to another subject.

"We're getting married as soon as possible, and I'll need a witness." She glanced hesitantly at Honey. "Would you be my witness?"

Honey rose and came around the table. She leaned over and hugged Emily tight. "I may not agree with what you're doing, but I'm there for you. Whatever you need, just say the word." For a moment, she stared at Emily, then smoothed back her hair. "Be sure this is what you want. Once it's done, it's hard to undo."

"I'm sure." As sure as she could be under the circumstances anyway. Tears stung Emily's eyes. She could always count on Honey. "Thanks."

"Are you going to tell Jess?"

Emily hadn't given any thought to calling her halfbrother. "Do you think I should?"

Pushing a long strand of blond hair behind her ear, Honey propped her hip against the table and crossed her arms over the bodice of her blue blouse. "He'll be hurt if he finds out any other way. You know he always feels as if he's left out of family matters. Why give him another chance to misconstrue your reasons?"

"I guess you're right. I'll call him when I get

home.'' She never looked forward to conversations with Jess. They'd never been close, not that she hadn't tried. There was just something about him that naturally kept people at arm's length, which was probably what accounted for his choice of the isolated life of a forest ranger.

Honey smiled and strolled to the open window overlooking Danny's play area. Pushing the sheer, white lace aside, she peered out at her son. Seemingly satisfied that he was okay, she dropped the curtain and turned back to Emily.

"So, did Kat ever tell you why he suddenly decided to reappear after so long?"

Shaking her head, Emily gazed past Honey. Through the filmy curtain, she could see Danny pushing a bright red truck around in circles while making noises like a gasoline engine. "No. And I didn't ask. I know he's hell-bent on fixing the house up and selling it, but beyond that—" She shrugged.

"Well, one thing for sure, he'll make pretty babies." Honey smirked at Emily.

Caught off guard by her sister's comment, Emily smirked back, while her mind replayed the way Kat filled out his T-shirt and jeans. "He certainly will," she murmured.

"Oh? Do I hear something in my sister's voice that might be interpreted as attraction?" Honey touched Emily's hand. "Be careful, Em. I don't want you hurt. We both know that men are not the best bet when it comes to being relied on. Kat's spent most of his life wandering around the country. And no one seems to know why.''

Emily had thought about that very aspect of Kat's life after he had left, and could find no answers. One thing she had figured out from some of his fleeting pained expressions whenever he spoke about the house, was that he'd been running from something and that something had hurt him. Memories of his parents' death? or something more? Actually, she didn't want to know. It was none of her business. Getting too close to Kat emotionally was something she intended to avoid.

Still, she couldn't totally disregard the helplessness she experienced at the idea of him hurting in any way. Even when she reminded herself that he'd voluntarily cut himself from her life, the feeling remained. Old habits evidently died harder than she'd thought.

"Miss Emily?"

Emily roused from her thoughts to find Tess, Amanda's Irish, self-proclaimed cook, standing next to her, holding out a tray of blackened cookies. Emily smiled and took one, absently biting into the hard surface. When her teeth didn't penetrate, she stopped, removed it from her mouth and looked at Honey for an explanation.

Her sister hid a smile. "Tess is experimenting with a new recipe."

"Me sister sent it from Texas," Tess offered by way of completing Honey's explanation. "She says she won a blue ribbon at the county fair with it last month. I'm trying to improve on it and plan on entering it meself in our fair." She clucked her tongue and frowned at the plate. "This batch cooked a tad too long, I'm thinking. I'll have to work on me timing." Her cheery, flour-spattered, Irish face broke into a broad grin. "Can't have me little sister getting the edge on me, now, can I?"

"Why not?" Honey cut in. "My sister's been getting the edge on me for years."

Emily ignored her sister's remark and studied the black wafer in her hand. It closely resembled something the Rangers might knock around on the ice. "Maybe a nice cup of tea to go with it?"

"Oh! Faith! Now, what was I thinking. Of course, you can't be enjoying a good biscuit without a cuppa tea to dunk it in." Tess sat down the plate of cookies and hurried off to the kitchen. "I'll have a pot brewed in no time."

Soaking the cookie was more what Emily had in mind.

"If you play your cards right, you'll make your escape before she comes back with the tea and you're forced to eat that thing." Honey nodded toward the cookie.

Standing and tucking the cookie, along with several more to keep from hurting Tess's feelings, into her jacket pocket, Emily smiled at Honey. "I don't understand why Amanda keeps her on."

Honey rose to walk Emily to the door. "First of all, she hasn't a clue that she's a terrible cook. Secondly, and most importantly, Amanda and I don't have the heart to stop her." She swung Emily to face her, her hands resting on her sister's shoulders. "Which goes to prove that sometimes you just have to make the best of an awkward situation. Who knows, things could turn out wonderful and really surprise you.''

''Sure, and the Gourmet Fairy is going to come down in the middle of the night and turn Tess into the next Julia Child.'' Honey laughed, but Emily found no humor in this conversation.

Her situation with Kat could hardly be described as just awkward. Disastrous was more like it. And how did she go about making a good situation out of a fiasco in the making?

Chapter Five

Emily stared at the bride looking back at her from the mirror in Amanda's spare room. She looked terrified, and with good reason—she was—from the top of her flowered headband to the tips of her white satin heels.

"You sure clean up nice, kid." Honey's soft voice came from behind her.

Shifting her gaze from her own reflection, she zeroed in on her sister's face peering over her shoulder. "If you go for the deer-in-the-headlights look."

"All brides are nervous. And under these particular circumstances, I'd say you have good reason to be a bit edgy." Honey held out a small nosegay of white daisies, yellow buttercups and wild blue asters. "Kat sent these for you. There's a note."

Emily took the note and slowly unfolded the paper. Nervously biting down on her bottom lip, she read Kat's words. "Hothouse flowers just didn't seem right for you, so I picked these from the meadow and had the florist arrange them into a bouquet. See you in a bit, Squirt. Kat. PS—Quit gnawing on your bottom lip. I promise, everything will be fine.''

"Damn him!'' Emily tossed the note aside and clutched at the bouquet.

Honey snatched up the note. "What did he say?''

"Nothing. I just hate that he's being so nice about this whole thing. I hate that I trapped him into this mess, and I hate that it has to be this way.'' Emily fingered a white daisy petal. "He knows me so well, Honey. He hasn't forgotten anything.'' She raised her gaze to Honey's. "So, why do *I* feel like I'm marrying a familiar stranger?''

Honey sat beside her on the edge of the bed. "Because you are. You've got a history, but it's a history of childhood. This adult Kat is the result of sixteen years that he wasn't a part of your life. He's changed, you've changed.''

Emily shook her head. "He's changed, but don't you see—I haven't. If I had, he wouldn't be able to read me so well. It's as if he can see inside my head sometimes. And…inside my heart at others.''

"And is that so bad? Em, listen to me.'' She touched her finger to Emily's chin and turned her to face her. "Marrying a man who truly knows you is so much better than marrying a man who *thinks* he knows you and doesn't have a clue as to what's in your heart.''

Emily turned away. She knew Honey was referring to her own marriage to Stan. But that didn't help Emily. Her relationship with Kat differed in so many ways from Honey's with Stan. Besides, there's a lot to be said for a man not being able to see into your heart, especially when you're no longer sure what it will reveal.

Standing, Honey touched Emily's shoulder. "I have to go downstairs and check on things. You gonna be okay?"

Nodding, Emily pulled herself together and sat straighter. This was silly. She'd made her bed, as Rose would say, now she had to lie in it. "I'm fine. Just a case of pre-wedding jitters." She forced herself to smile reassuringly at her sister, who looked so lovely in her powder-blue dress. She squeezed her fingers. "Thanks."

Honey kissed her cheek, then left the room to see to the guests they'd invited. Emily still wasn't too sure about Honey's plan to make the divorce less suspect by asking a few friends to attend and at least give the appearance of a real wedding. But the ceremony would begin in a few minutes and it was much too late to worry about that now.

Honey had done a wonderful job planning the wedding on such short notice and Emily didn't have the heart to tell her that white dresses, flowers, a minister and a reception only made her feel more like a cheat than ever.

And speaking of cheating, she still couldn't feel good about what Kat was doing for her, even if she'd been the one to introduce the subject. Marriage was such an enormous step, even for two people who loved each other. She and Kat didn't have that much going for them.

But this isn't a permanent arrangement. The

voice of her conscience brought everything back into perspective.

This marriage was a temporary business arrangement. She had no illusions about it being any more than that, nor did she want it to be. She glanced down at the bouquet of wildflowers that Kat had gone to such trouble to get for her. It seemed that Kat would have to be reminded of that fact from time to time. She caressed the smooth petals. Still, it had been a very sweet thing for him to do.

KAT STOOD next to a makeshift alter in front of the fireplace, Dave Thornton at his side as best man. His trousers fluttered against his shaking legs. This was ridiculous. He was getting married to a woman he'd known all his life. What did he have to be nervous about?

Oh, not much, a little voice in the back of his head offered. *You're taking on the responsibilities of a wife and a child. Okay, so you've known Emily since childhood. There's a little matter of sixteen years and a whole growing process that you haven't been privy to as far as Emily is concerned. What made you think you could do this? This isn't just a case of saying I dos and getting back to life. This is a major life-style change. This is sharing a home with someone, something you haven't done since...*

No, he wasn't going there. Not today. He had enough to worry about without delving into his past.

Maybe he should just walk out now, while he still could. No. He couldn't do that to Emily. He'd given his word. He'd promised to marry her and father her child and by damn, he'd do it, even if it meant....

The music started and Dave nudged him. "Here comes your bride."

Kat glanced toward the doorway. Just inside the arch stood Emily. His breath caught in his throat. He couldn't recall seeing Emily look so beautiful. That the movement of her flowers matched the trembling in his legs made him smile. She smiled back, tentatively, but no less a smile.

He wanted to reach out to her, tell her what they were doing was good and right. Tell her she'd never be sorry. Tell her.... What?

In a moment, he was going to promise to love, honor and obey this woman until he died, knowing that in a few months, he'd be expected to break that promise. But Emily would be making the same promise, and he knew how Emily felt about breaking promises. For reasons he didn't want to delve into, the thought lightened his spirits tremendously.

Emily walked slowly toward Kat, her gaze pinned to the carnation in his lapel. If she looked at him, she was sure she'd back out of their deal. She kept her mind centered on the baby. Think about the baby. But thinking about the baby only brought to mind how she'd have to go about acquiring the baby. Then her hands began to shake even harder.

Suddenly, she was standing beside Kat, his large, warm hand holding hers. She heard her voice promise to love, honor and obey Kat until death parted them. Emily had never made a promise in her life she didn't fully intend to keep. That she did now sickened her.

"I now pronounce you man and wife." The minister's voice cut through her thoughts. "You may kiss your bride."

Kat turned to her, his eyes dark and filled with some emotion she found it hard to read. "Too late to back out now, Squirt."

Her last thought before his lips covered hers was, *Oh, god, what have I done?*

EMILY FOLDED the white lace suit and placed it in a box lined with tissue paper. As she stared down at the suit for a minute, it hit home that she was now a married woman.

"Mrs. Rian Madison." The sound of her new name brought a nervous smile to her lips.

Gently covering the garment with another sheet of tissue, she replaced the lid, then slipped it onto the top shelf of her bedroom closet.

When Honey had suggested it, Emily hadn't been sure about wearing a white dress for the wedding ceremony. Not because of any old-fashioned interpretations about virginal white, but because she knew this wasn't a real wedding and it made her feel like a fraud to pretend otherwise. She'd have been just as happy wearing something from her closet. But Honey had insisted on both the dress and the elaborate ceremony, and Emily had neither the heart nor the energy to argue.

However the expression on Kat's face when he first saw her had done things to her insides she was still trying to get under control. It hadn't helped that Kat's dark suit and white shirt against his tanned complexion made him look like a pirate come to claim his bounty.

Thoughts of Kat sent her to the window to see if he'd come back yet with his belongings. She pushed aside the curtain and checked below. The driveway was empty. Happy for the extended time to get used to the idea of Kat living under her roof and what that would soon entail, she dropped the curtain and headed for the bathroom.

Staring into the mirror, she removed the makeup Honey had applied for the ceremony. As Emily dropped the soiled tissue into the wastepaper basket, she reminded herself to make room in the medicine cabinet for Kat's toiletries. She stopped dead, face-to-face with the finality of the day. Whether or not she liked it, Kat was moving into her life and her home as no other man ever had.

The last time she'd shared the house with a man, he'd controlled her life. She made a silent vow that Kat would not take up where her father had left off.

Quickly, she finished clearing the space, then headed for the kitchen. After the last few hours, she could use the shoring up of coffee that, as Rose claimed, could support a spoon—vertically.

LATER THAT NIGHT, after he'd moved his belongings from the car to the spare room, Kat came into the living room where Emily was staring at the TV. Though she'd heard his movements, she'd intentionally avoided watching him. It would be just one more thing to remind her of the finality of her own actions.

"I'm going to bed."

His words brought Emily's nerves back to alert. "Not me." She grabbed the remote and began surfing the channels. "There's a show on I've been waiting to see."

"Oh. What is it? Maybe I'll watch it with you."

"No. You wouldn't be interested. It's a chick flick. You know, gushy and romantic." Emily kept her eyes on the TV, wishing he'd continue upstairs to bed—alone.

"What makes you think I'm not interested in romance?"

Emily never let on she heard him. The last thing she wanted to discuss with Kat Madison was romance.

After she'd had time to calm down following the pre-wedding jitters, it had occurred to her, as the day wore on, that the time was drawing closer when Kat would expect her to share his bed. Her nerves had gotten tighter and tighter all day. By now, she had to fight to keep from screaming that she'd made a terrible mistake. She couldn't do this.

She could feel Kat's gaze on her. She concentrated on finding something on TV that resembled her fictitious show. Nothing but war movies, westerns and infomercials flickered across the screen.

"Are you sure tonight's the night it'll be on? I don't see anything like you described." Kat continued to stare at her.

She leaned forward and pressed harder on the remote buttons, willing the TV to cooperate in her lie. A third pass through all the channels brought nothing new. She gave up. "Maybe it was another night. Well, you might as well go to bed. I'm not tired. I'm gonna stay up for a while and…" she set down the remote and grabbed for a copy of a horse breeders' magazine "…read. There was an article in here that—"

"Em." Kat had come to sit next to her. She froze. He took the magazine from her, laid it on the coffee table, then slipped his curled finger under her chin. She raised her gaze to meet his. "When you are ready and not before. I promise. Trust me. Okay?"

She looked into his dark eyes, searching for sincerity. It was there, shining back at her like a beacon. She swallowed hard and nodded. "Okay."

His reassuring smile wove its way through her bloodstream, heating her body like a blowtorch. She couldn't look away. Her gaze dropped to his mouth. His full, mouth. His kissable mouth waiting for—

Emily almost pulled away, but he must have read what she'd been thinking.

"You want to know, too, don't you, Em? Well, so do I, so let's satisfy our curiosity."

She willed herself to pull back, but it was too late. His soft, seductive voice had her mesmerized.

"It won't hurt, Em. Not just once." Slowly, he leaned closer, eating up the tiny distance separating their lips. "Just once."

The first contact of his lips startled Emily with the softness. His lips shouldn't be soft and seductive. A man's lips should be hard and demanding. But they weren't and Emily couldn't fight what they were doing to her. She leaned forward.

Kat never released her chin, nor did he draw her into his embrace. The only places they touched were his fingertip under her chin and their lips. If he had just hauled her into his arms and kissed her senseless, it would have been easier for Emily to resist. But this tender whisper of a kiss scrambled her thoughts. To pull away was impossible.

When his lips left hers, she experienced a mixture of regret and gladness. Then they were back, nibbling and exploring, coaxing her to open for him. Though the kiss hadn't gained in strength, it had grown in sensuality. Emily went fluid, nerveless, boneless. She swayed toward him.

Kat pulled back. "I guess I'd better go to bed." He stood, then stared down at her for a long time, as if assessing something.

Emily suddenly felt inadequate. She hadn't had much practice kissing. Maybe he'd found her lacking. Maybe he'd found her inexperience distasteful.

"We need to forget what just happened," she said, trying to keep her voice steady and her eyes averted. "This arrangement is business, nothing more."

When Kat didn't move, she glanced up at him towering above her, his face blank, his eyes shielded behind an expressionless glaze. "I'll remember," he said, then turned toward the stairs. She heard his foot hit the first stair, then nothing. "Can you forget?" Then he continued on his way to the spare room.

Emily sat motionless for a long time, her fingers caressing the spot on her lips where the taste of Kat's kiss still lingered. Forget? She'd never admit it to him, but she had the feeling she'd take that kiss to her grave.

KAT PULLED into the driveway, his truck bed loaded with grocery bags filled with meat, veggies, milk, eggs and fresh fruit.

Honey's black-haired son sat on the porch cradling one of the brown-and-white puppies Kat had seen scampering around the yard. Since Danny hadn't been at the wedding this would be their first meeting. The kid reminded him of Emily.

"Hi."

"Hi there. What's your name?"

"Danny. What's y-y-yours?"

"Kat."

The boy scrunched up his nose. "C-c-cat? Like a kitty c-c-cat?"

Kat laughed. "Not exactly." He glanced at the bags in the truck. "How would you like a job?"

"You gonna p-p-pay me?"

What the kid lacked in subtlety he made up for with his business sense. "Of course. How about a dollar?"

Danny's eyes widened. He put the puppy down. "Sure. W-w-what do I have to do?"

"Help me carry in the groceries."

"Gee. I help my mom do that all the t-t-time and she never pays me." Danny hurried toward Kat. "I need to see the money first."

He held out a hand that could have used a confrontation with a bar of soap and some water. Kat dug in his pocket and pulled out a dollar bill, surprised that Danny's stutter seemed to have all but disappeared. He placed it in Danny's hand and smiled at the way the boy examined it. "It's real."

"I never had this much money all for m-m-myself before." He folded the bill neatly, then stuffed it in the pocket of his jeans. He looked up at Kat with large, dark eyes. "You know my aunt Emily?"

"Yup." Kat lifted the bag containing only a loaf of bread from the truck and placed it in Danny's outstretched arms. "I used to play with her when she was about your age." He tucked a bag in the crook of each arm and grabbed one in each hand. They walked together toward the house.

Danny managed to hold open the door. "Are you gonna give Aunt Emily a b-b-baby?"

While Kat fumbled to keep his grip on the bags, he searched for an answer.

"Daniel Matthew Logan!"

Both males looked up. In the doorway stood Kat's blond sister-in-law, hands on her hips, a disapproving gaze centered on Kat's young employee. "You apologize for that question this instant. And then you mind your own business, young man."

"He's inquisitive, Honey. Just like his aunt was at that age." Kat sidled past his new sister-in-law and deposited the bags on the kitchen table.

"That's no excuse for rudeness."

Kat looked around the kitchen. "Where's Emily?"

"In the horse barn. She said she'd be up for lunch in a minute. One of the horses pulled a muscle and she's checking it out with the vet." Honey took the bag from her son and peeked into it before setting it on the table. "Fruit, veggies, milk?" She glanced at Kat. "Does my sister know you're trying to poison her?"

"Not yet. It's a surprise."

"You g-g-gonna k-k-kill Aunt Emily?"

Danny's stutter had come back, but the child's face had taken on a look that reminded Kat very much of his defiant wife. No mistake. He was ready to do battle for his beloved aunt.

"No. I'm trying to get her to eat good food. She's the one who'll look at it like poison."

"Oh." Danny dug his hand in his pocket. "Look, M-m-mommy. Kat paid me to c-c-carry the groceries for him. I g-g-got a whole dollar."

"*Uncle* Kat."

"Can we go to the s-s-store on the way home?" Danny went on as if he hadn't heard his mother.

Honey threw Kat a look that said she wasn't happy that he'd paid Danny to do a task that he should have done as a courtesy. She sighed. "We'll see. Why don't you round up the puppies? Chuck said they need to be back in the barn so their mommy can feed them lunch."

"Ok-k-kay." Danny shoved his money back in his pocket, then ran for the front door. He stopped short. "Mr. K-k-kat?"

"Yes?"

"I l-l-like you."

Kat felt a smile growing deep inside him. "Then why don't you call me Uncle Kat?"

"Ok-k-kay. Uncle Kat." Danny grinned, then scooted out the door.

"There's hope for you, Kat Madison." Honey grabbed some vegetables from a bag and carried them to the refrigerator.

"For what?" Kat filled his arms with milk, eggs and other perishables and followed her.

"Taking on this business of being a father. It's not an easy job, but I think you'll do just fine." She held open the refrigerator door for him. "And thanks for the way you handled Danny's problem. He's been missing a man's influence in his life." She smiled at Kat. "You're gonna be good for Emily, too."

"That's the nicest thing anyone has ever said to me, Mrs. Logan." He returned to the bags of groceries. "But if I don't get your sister to eat something besides peanut butter and banana sandwiches, our kid will be born with a long tail and a craving for nuts."

"Kat." Honey laid a hand on his sleeve. "I was dead-set against this crazy scheme of Emily's. I did everything I could to talk her out of it." She gently squeezed his arm. "But something tells me, if she thinks this will be easy, my little sister is in for a rude awakening." She winked, then her expression became serious. "I didn't get a chance to say so yesterday, but thanks for helping Emily out. Not many men would do what you're doing."

He patted her hand. "You know what a pushover I am for your sister."

"I know what a pushover you *used* to be. I wasn't sure you'd still want to get involved with Em's problems. She can be a handful."

Kat smiled. "Don't I know it?" His mind darted to last night and that kiss. If they'd kept kissing, he'd have pulled her into his arms and found out just how much of a handful she was.

"What's going on here?"

Both of them turned to the back door. Emily stood just inside the kitchen, her gaze taking in the bags sitting everywhere.

"Kat went grocery shopping."

"We didn't need groceries. I went shopping two days ago." Emily looked into the nearest bag.

"If I'm going to cook, then I needed certain ingredients that we didn't have." Kat glanced toward Honey, busily trying to hide the smirk curving her lips, then he started loading the meat into the freezer. "Man can't subsist on bananas and peanut butter alone, you know."

Once more, Emily felt control of her life slipping from her grasp. Anger boiling inside her like a rising summer storm, she faced Kat. "Who said you're cooking? And what right do you have coming in here and rearranging things to your liking?"

Kat put a large roast beef in the freezer, closed the door, then walked to where Emily stood. He looked her directly in the eye. "I am the father of our future child. That gives me every right to make sure you have the chance to eat good food and take care of yourself. Now whether or not you do is up to you, but I need decent meals. As for cooking, if you'd like to do it, be my guest. However, since last I heard you didn't know the difference between a saucepan and a frypan, that leaves me.''

Guilt took the fire out of her anger. Damn him! There he went being thoughtful and logical again. How was she supposed to fight him, if he kept being nice to her and using common sense against her? And as far as eating went, she liked healthy food. She just didn't have a clue how to convert it from the raw state to the edible state. ''Well, I hope you know how to cook all this stuff you bought.''

He smiled down at her and then kissed her forehead. ''No problem, Squirt. Just tell me what you want for supper and I'll cook it.''

A devilish streak goaded Emily on. ''Anything?''

''Anything.''

Emily glanced at her sister. ''Lasagna.''

''Emily!'' Honey glared at her.

''He did say anything, Honey.'' She looked wide-eyed at Kat, but she could tell by his expression he wasn't buying into her innocence. ''Didn't you? Or do you forget that quickly?''

''I don't forget anything. Lasagna it is.'' Then he centered his burning gaze on her. ''What about you, Squirt? How's your memory?'' The suggestive quality in his low, taunting tone captured Emily in its grip, and for a moment, she had to fight to keep at bay memories of the night before and the kiss they'd shared. His smile deepened and spread to his eyes.

That's exactly what he'd intended. Even knowing that, she still couldn't budge.

"Well, I can see you two have things under control, so I'll be running along." Honey's amused voice filtered through the sensuality surrounding Emily. "No, Danny and I can't stay for lunch, but thanks for asking. No, don't try to change my mind." She paused. "That's okay. I can see myself out. I can— Oh, hells bells."

As if drifting to her through a heavy fog, Emily heard the front door open and close, then Honey calling to Danny, then her car starting and moving down the driveway. Still Emily could not tear her attention from Kat's hot gaze. Worse yet, she found herself wishing he'd kiss her again—this time like he meant it.

Chapter Six

Emily clung to the rail of the white board fence and watched a mare and her new colt scamper around the close-cropped grass. But her mind wasn't on the horses. The sound of hammering drifting across the field consumed her thoughts.

Two days had passed since Kat had taken over the cooking and Emily had to admit, she enjoyed eating healthy. His lasagna had been delicious, and he had popped some wonders out of the breadmaker that would make Rose green with envy. He'd told her he'd learned to cook as a matter of survival. She wondered what else he'd done to survive.

She knew so little about this new Kat, the Kat she'd married. Though they'd tried, they hadn't been able to recapture their old camaraderie and, for the most part, they engaged in meaningless small talk, staying safely away from any mention of the baby. Until they did become friends again, Emily wasn't sure she could just climb into his bed and make a baby. But how did she make that happen?

"Miss Emily?"

The sound of her foreman's voice brought Emily out of her blue funk.

"Yes?"

"You wanted to see me?"

Although Emily had planned on not spreading the news of her marriage far and wide so that later, after the divorce, there would be fewer explanations to make, she had to tell her employees that Kat and she had gotten married.

"Kat Madison and I were married yesterday."

Chuck's face glowed. "Congratulations, Miss Emily." Then he turned red with embarrassment. "I guess you're not suppose' to say that to the bride. Some say it's like congratulating her on finding a man."

Emily hoped her mental flinch didn't show. "Thank you, Chuck. I wanted also to assure you that nothing will change. The farm will go on as it always has. Kat knows horses, too, so if you have any problems, just call him. Other than that, he'll stay out of your way." And mine, she added silently but hopefully. When Chuck didn't move away, she frowned. "Something wrong?"

He stepped beside her and rested one booted foot next to hers on the rail. "I was just wonderin'. Since Midnight Lady is close to her time, are you sure you want me to take my vacation now?" He pushed his hat back off his forehead and swiped with a faded red bandana handkerchief at the dots of moisture gathered there. "I can always go after she has her foal."

"Do you see any problems?"

"No. She's new at this, but she's a healthy, fairly docile mare. Shouldn't be any problems."

She patted the shoulder of his blue shirt. "I'd rather you go now than wait until later. We'll have four new mares coming in week after next. I need you here then."

Chuck pulled his hat back down to shade his eyes. "Then I'll be leaving right after dinner."

"Fine. Have a good time, Chuck."

She watched him saunter away, the epitome of something out of an old western, but as indispensable to her as.... The hammering started again, then silence, then more hammering. An idea struck her. Maybe she could give a little nudge to helping renew the friendship between Kat and herself. Maybe then she'd be able to get on with the business of getting pregnant. Not even to herself did she want to admit that more than that drove her to seek out Kat's company.

"HEY, MADISON. I'm looking for a job. Any openings?"

Kat glanced down at the ground. He grabbed the crown of the roof to keep from falling off. Below him stood Emily, decked out like a female version of Tim "The Toolman" Taylor, complete with tool belt, work boots, jeans and a low-cut orange tank top. In her hand, she brandished a hammer, just as if she knew what to do with it.

It pleased him that she had sought him out. However, he had a clear recollection of the last time Emily had a hammer in her hand. They'd built a tree house in the west pasture. After she'd smacked his thumb with the hammer, it had taken months for his nail to grow back. Was he ready to risk that again?

"Well? You hiring or not?"

"Hang on. Let me come down there." Being able to talk to her better from the ground didn't figure into his decision. It just beat the hell out of falling from a thirty-foot roof peak because he was trying not to look down her gaping tank top.

Carefully, Kat worked his way down the roof to where the aluminum ladder leaned against it, then climbed down to Emily.

"Well? You gonna give me a job?"

Her eyes sparkled up at him. Kat swallowed hard. Maybe he'd have been safer on the roof. "Depends on your qualifications, fella. And if memory serves—" he held up his thumb with the still deformed nail "—hammering isn't one of them."

Emily frowned. "Good grief, Kat, that was years ago. I was just a kid. Now, what about that job?"

"You belong to a union?"

Her face lost its humor. "Since about two days ago." She touched his arm. "That's one of the reasons I came over to help. We've been avoiding each other. That's not gonna help me get used to the idea of making a baby with you."

A hard ball of disappointment formed in Kat's stomach. She'd only done this because of the baby. He'd had a faint hope that she'd sought him out for other reasons. He didn't know why that mattered, but it did—a lot.

"Okay. Get your cute little tush up there. Be careful."

Emily started up the ladder with him right behind her. Her foot slipped on the rung and he grabbed her bottom to steady her. His hands burned where the fabric of her jeans rested against them, knowing what lay just beneath the worn denim. She gripped the side rails of the ladder, then glanced over her shoulder at him.

He grinned and pulled his hands away. "Sorry."

He wasn't really sorry at all. He'd enjoyed it. And truth be known, she probably had too.

She stepped off the ladder and he followed. The roof was steep and very high. She glanced down. Maybe this was a mistake. Maybe she should have waited until she could help him with something at ground level.

With his forefinger, Kat raised her chin. "First rule is don't look down."

She nodded and kept her gaze averted from the edge. "What do I do?"

The words had barely passed her lips when her foot slipped. She struggled to keep her balance and grabbed for a bucket sitting on the ladder's paint-can platform. The bucket teetered, then fell over the side. The sound of metallic rain followed. Carefully looking down, she could see galvanized roofing nails scattered over the ground.

She glanced at Kat. He was also looking down. "Sorry," she offered.

He shook his head, then guided her to where he'd stopped working about six feet from the peak. "No problem. I have more in my nail apron.'' Pushing her to a squatting position, then to her knees, he handed her a shingle. "Watch me.''

No hardship there, she thought.

Carefully and slowly, he instructed her in the art of applying shingles. She absorbed his instructions, even though she still wasn't sure exactly what she was doing. "Think you can do it?''

She nodded and grabbed a shingle. Slipping it into place and overlapping it as he had done, she took the handful of nails he passed her, put them into her tool belt, keeping one out. Holding it with one hand, while Kat watched, she pounded the nail into place. She turned to him and grinned, then repeated the procedure. When she'd finished, she leaned back to admire her first shingle.

"Terrific. Looks like I have myself a partner.''

For reasons she couldn't fathom and wasn't about to explore further, Kat's praise filled Emily with uncontrollable contentment. When they were children, Kat had always been the one there first with applause for her accomplishments. Her father's reaction had typically been a nod. She'd forgotten how good it was to be appreciated, but this feeling went beyond mere pleasure in his approval. This went to something that a woman feels for a man whose opinions matter beyond mere praise. Quickly, Emily grabbed another shingle.

For a time, they worked silently. Emily worked a bit below Kat, so she had an unobstructed view of his bare back. After losing her balance once or twice, it didn't take her long to realize that dwelling on the seductive ripple of his back muscles every time he moved could be hazardous to her health. She averted her gaze and concentrated on the slabs of tar paper and grit.

Admiring Kat was not why she'd come here, anyway, although it wasn't a bad by-product. She'd come to learn more about the man that she'd once known so well she could tell when he would take his next breath.

"So, have you been working as a carpenter all these years?"

Kat kept working, but mumbled what sounded like "off and on."

"Where've you been working?"

"Around."

His succinct replies grated on her nerves. She plunged on. "Last I remember you were hell-bent on becoming a vet."

"Yup." Kat wasn't going to tell her that he'd completed courses at some of the major veterinary schools around the country while looking for his birth parents. Or that he'd finally taken three years off from the search and finished a degree at Cornell, a few hours north of here. Or how many times he'd thought about coming home to see her and then decided not to for fear of hurting her.

He turned slowly and carefully to face her. "We're never gonna get done here if you keep asking questions."

"I was just trying to get to know you better."

"Getting to know me isn't why we're here." His shortened tone left no room for discussion.

"How else will we get comfortable with each other?" She glared at him for a moment, then slung a shingle into place. Just as her hammer descended, the shingle slipped from her grasp. Kat reached in front of her to grab it. The hammer slammed into his finger.

"Son of a...." Grabbing his finger, he howled in pain.

"Kat. Oh, I'm sorry. Are you all right? Can I do something?"

"No...my fault...shouldn't have had...my hand there." His voice choked with pain, he held his finger.

For what seemed like forever, Emily sat helplessly by, waiting for his pain to subside. Kat in pain was one thing she'd never learned to handle well. The same feelings she'd had the day she'd whacked his thumb in the tree house washed over her. Nausea threatened to claim her. She swallowed hard.

Finally, he smiled weakly at her. "Listen, it's almost lunchtime. Before I left this morning, I made a sub and a salad. How about if I clean up here and you go get everything out for lunch?"

"*A* sub and *a* salad? Is there enough for two?"

He smiled through the pain and leaned close enough so she could feel the warm brush of his breath against her cheeks. He kissed her. Quick and without passion, but no less devastating to Emily's peace of mind. "Sure, Squirt. We can share."

"Oh." Still shaken by the feel of his lips against hers, she looked away, then rose carefully and started toward the ladder. "Are you sure you'll be okay?"

"Yes. It's better already."

She could tell by the way his brows drew together that it was not better, but she also recalled how embarrassing it had been for him to admit to being hurt when they were kids. Men weren't supposed to show pain. Wasn't that what her father had told her brother, Jesse, over and over?

She nodded and finished her descent from the roof. Before she walked through the trees, she looked up at Kat and smiled. "See you in a few minutes," she called.

Kat waved back. As soon as she disappeared into the trees, he grabbed his finger again. It had already started to turn a disgusting shade of purple and every time the blood pulsed to it, it felt as if the end would blow off. Gads, for a little woman, she sure could wield a hammer.

He'd loved having her with him and was inordinately pleased with her efforts to bring them closer, but they'd have to come up with a better way. A way that didn't involve sharp objects or blunt instruments or questions that he couldn't answer.

"LET ME AT LEAST HELP with the dishes," Em protested as Kat winced after trying to pick up a dirty supper plate.

"You look tired," Kat said. "I'll finish up here. Why don't you go into the living room and see if you can find something on TV worth us spending an hour or so glued to the set?" With his good hand, he piled the plates and carried them to the dish-washer. "Maybe an old Bogart movie?"

Emily smiled as she left the kitchen, recalling her love of old movies and his dislike of them when they were younger. It had surprised her that he'd made the suggestion. In the living room, she absently ran the TV through its paces. Nothing appealed to her, but that could be because she was still feeling very guilty about having hurt Kat. She didn't blame him for not wanting her help with supper or doing the supper dishes. She was an accident looking for a place to happen. She'd probably stab him with a bread knife, and he'd bleed to death before her eyes.

And she was going to have a small baby to take care of soon. The thought of what she might do inadvertently to a baby had the power to send chills through her.

Perhaps it was the hopelessness of her situation, perhaps just a collection of the events of the last few weeks, but suddenly Emily found herself fighting back tears. She didn't cry. She never cried. Damn! Not now, when Kat could walk in at any minute and catch her. What was wrong with her? Her emotions had gone haywire. This wasn't supposed to happen until after she got pregnant. If she was this bad now, she'd be a basket case while she carried her child.

Though she fought valiantly, she lost. Hot tears rolled down her cheeks, and soon she had her face buried in a throw pillow, sobbing her heart out.

Kat could hear Emily's soft sobs before he got all the way into the room. He knew she'd been having nervous attacks about the prospect of sharing his bed, but he hadn't realized until now just how much they'd been affecting her. He hurried to the couch and gathered her in his arms.

"What is it, Em? What's wrong? Talk to me."

"I'm going to be a terrible mother," she wailed into his shoulder. "I can't even hammer a nail without hurting someone."

"That's not true." He rubbed her back and laid his face against her sweet-smelling hair. "You'll make a wonderful mother. "

She drew back, hiccupped, then sniffed. "Really?"

He kissed her nose. "Really."

"But I don't know anything about babies."

"Neither do I." He placed his palm against her wet cheek. "We'll learn together. Okay?"

She nodded. "I just want our baby to be happy and healthy and know we love her."

Kat wondered if she was aware that she had just included him in the raising of their child. Or that, for the first time, she'd referred to their yet-to-be-conceived child as *our baby*. Warmth spread through him. Was he winning Em over?

Winning her over for what? What exactly did he want from Em? What were his real feelings for this woman who had filled his head for days and had wormed her way beneath his shell of emotional self-protection from the first day he'd seen her again?

He gazed down into her tear-streaked face and felt his heart twist in response to the anguish he saw there. Anguish for a child yet to become a reality.

With his thumb, he wiped away the traces of moisture crisscrossing her cheeks. How soft Em's skin was, considering the time she spent in the sun and weather. Like soft, luxuriant suede. And her eyes. They shone up at him like two huge green jewels.

How had he survived for all these years without his friend, his buddy? And was she still his buddy? Or had she become more?

His gaze dropped to her mouth, slightly swollen from being bitten, her bottom lip still trembling as if she were on the verge of more tears. Her gaze searched his face, asking him for something. What? He read the silent answer in her expression. Em wanted what he did. To replay the kiss they'd shared that first night.

From deep down inside him surged an uncontrollable need to feel her lips touch his again. He leaned forward. She met him halfway.

Their lips melded in a kiss that had all the power to lay naked emotions Kat hadn't ever experienced before. Emotions that confirmed that he regarded Emily as more than a friend. Much more.

This time, instead of allowing distance to separate their bodies, he pulled her into his embrace, needing to feel her against him, perhaps to assure himself she was real and not just another of his fantasies. His daydreams of holding Emily and kissing her fell far short of the real thing.

The surge of sensation started at Emily's toes and catapulted upward, taking her into a world of sensuality she'd never known existed. She slipped her arms around Kat's neck and pulled his mouth down on hers, wanting all he could give.

He slid his hand down her side and around her rib cage to cup her breast. A moan emerged from deep in her throat. She nestled into his hand. Oddly, sexuality wasn't the only emotion she was feeling. She felt secure, protected, cherished. She wanted this moment to go on forever. Never to leave the safety of Kat's arms.

He rained kisses down her face, her neck and her ears. He murmured endearments to her, things Kat had never said to her before. Things a man would say to a woman he planned on making his lover.

That thought had the effect of ice water on Emily. What was she thinking? This relationship was heading down the wrong road at an alarming speed. She had to put on the brakes, because if the way Kat was kissing her was any indication, *he* wasn't about to.

She jumped back, then quickly got to her feet, leaving Kat on the couch with a stricken look of surprise on his face.

"What...?"

"This is wrong. I told you, no emotional involvement."

"And what was that that just happened, Emily?" He stared a hole through her waiting for her answer, an answer she couldn't safely give herself.

"I don't know, but it can't happen again."

"It wasn't a commitment. It was two people sharing a tender moment."

Shaking her head, Emily tried to deny anything

beyond a purely sexual encounter. "Hormones. That's all that was, just hormones."

Kat laughed. "I can't deny that the hormones were playing a large role in what just happened, but it was more than that. You know it and I know it."

Kat continued to study Emily. The signs were all there. He'd been right. What had just happened between them involved a whole lot more than hormones. But he wasn't blind or insensitive. Emily wasn't ready to face anything that even came close to an emotional commitment.

To his utter shock, he realized why. Emily was terrified. He'd never known her to be afraid of anything. He'd seen her tackle some of the orneriest horses that ever stepped onto her land, simply by letting them know who was boss. But horses and emotions were two entirely different things. Horses could be broken. Emotions happened with or without permission. If that kiss and her response were anything to go by, Emily's emotions had bolted beyond her control and she was running scared. Denial afforded her the safety she sought right now and he couldn't steal it from her. He let the subject die.

Slowly, he stood and moved toward the stairs. Then he stopped and turned toward her. "About you being afraid of taking care of the baby..."

She held a throw pillow in front of her, as if taking refuge behind it.

"Before you can take care of it, we need to make it." He gazed at her for a long moment before going on, picking words that would not frighten her more, but might help her past the next hurdle of their relationship. "It'll be your move. I won't go back on my word. But if you push me away every time I get near you…" He didn't need to finish. Her tormented expression told him she got the picture.

KAT'S WORDS followed Emily to her room. She knew he was right. Either she got past this absurd idea that if she went to bed with him she'd get emotionally involved or she'd end up homeless and childless. Lots of women went to bed with men they had no emotional involvement with. This was, after all, a modern society she lived in.

She flopped on her bed and stared out the window at the moon painting the landscape a bluish gray. Somehow, all of that land that lay beyond her bedroom window meant less than it had. What she'd come to need and want, even more than the land, was the child. And there was only one way to get it, if Kat was to be its father. It shocked her that she found the idea of anyone but Kat fathering her child as totally repugnant.

To avoid thinking along those lines, she went to her dresser and then began rifling through her nightgowns, looking for something Kat might find sexy and alluring.

Chapter Seven

Emily inspected the pitiful selection of nightwear spread over her bed: faded T-shirts, hand-me-down flannel shirts from Jess or her father, long flannel nightgowns for those nippy northern nights. Not one of them had a come-hither look a man would find irresistible. And, if she expected to share Kat's bed, she'd need something that would call out to him so he couldn't mistake what she had in mind.

Maybe Honey had something. She picked up the phone on her bedside table and dialed her sister's number.

"Mmmhullo."

"Honey? I need a sexy nightgown. Do you have one?"

Silence.

"Honey? Answer me." Impatience raised the volume of Emily's voice. "Honey, are you there?"

Another long silence followed, then, "As *here* as I ever get at…three forty-seven in the morning."

Emily's gaze shot to her alarm clock's glowing red numerals. "Good grief, Honey, I'm so sorry. Go back to sleep. I'll call you in the morning.'' She started to pull the receiver away from her ear.

''Emily Kingston, don't you dare hang up that phone! You can't call me at this hour, wake me up, ask me for a sexy nightgown, then just hang up and not tell me what the hell's going on.''

Emily hesitated.

''Emily? Do you hear me? Don't you hang up! I know where you live. I *will* come get you, and, trust me, it won't be a pretty sight.''

Oh, heck, she'd gone this far, she might as well go all the way. Keeping it locked in her head wouldn't make it go away or lessen her growing desire for her old playmate. She whispered into the phone, ''I need to go to bed with Kat.''

''I knew it!'' Honey's soft chuckle came through the receiver, building slowly until she was laughing so hard, Emily had to pull the phone away from her ear.

''This is not funny,'' she yelled toward the phone, then, realizing she might wake up Kat, she lowered her voice. ''Honey, this is serious.''

Her sister's laughter slowly subsided. ''I'm sorry, but you said that as if it was a state secret.''

''Well, it's certainly not something I want broadcast all over town.''

''Then you'd better not be seen with him in public, because what I saw going on between you two in your kitchen yesterday was like hanging a sign on you that said I Want To Jump Kat Madison's Bones.''

Emily recalled the heat that had passed between

her and Kat in the kitchen. She wasn't about to admit this to Honey, but if he'd pushed, she wasn't at all sure she'd have wanted to divert the intent she saw in his eyes.

"Don't be ridiculous. I called because, when I do decide to go ahead with this, I need a nightgown that doesn't look like I got it at the local thrift store."

"Yeah, right. At four in the morning, you're worried about being fashionably acceptable in a man's bed, just in case? Who are you trying to kid?"

Emily sighed. She could never fool Honey. "Okay, you win. So, do you have a nightgown?"

Honey yawned. "I can't help you, kid. I sleep in T-shirts and none of them are designed to excite anyone but the sandman. Don't you have anything you can alter into something presentable?"

Emily exhaled impatiently. "Even if I could sew, there's nothing."

Along with cooking, sewing had been something else she'd avoided while growing up. She wasn't sure why. Maybe because it made her undesirable wife material? A safety net? The idea that she'd made certain not to become involved with a man long ago by avoiding domestic skills set her back on her heels. Had she really been making an unconscious effort all these years to avoid emotional entanglements? And, if that were true, then why?

Honey's voice cut into her thoughts. "Why don't you just wait until tomorrow and go shopping?"

Emily glanced across the room into the oval, framed mirror that had hung in her room above the oak dresser since her childhood. Staring back at her was a woman she hardly recognized. "I guess so. Thanks. Go back to sleep."

Without waiting for Honey to say goodbye, Emily hung up the phone and walked to the mirror to inspect her reflection. She'd been looking at this face for twenty-nine years, yet...

She leaned closer, studying her features. Her eyes sparkled with a life she'd never noticed before. Her mouth seemed unusually full, as if begging to be kissed. But it was more than just a physical change that captured her attention. A new radiance surrounded her. The radiance of a woman in—

No, she wouldn't say it. She twisted away, blotting out the image of the woman in the mirror, the woman who forced her to look into places she didn't want to see, feel things she didn't want to feel, dared her to take risks she had no intention of taking.

She sank down on her bed, stunned into thought by this stranger she'd found hiding inside herself. Who was she? Where had she been for twenty-nine years? But more importantly, did her sudden emergence mean what Emily thought it did? Was she ready to risk a relationship with Kat? Had she been waiting for him all this time?

NOT CONCENTRATING on his work but glancing instead toward the house for signs of Emily had slowed Kat's progress to a near halt. He'd been on the roof for three hours and had managed to lay half a row of shingles.

Funny, she'd only worked with him for a short

time yesterday, but he missed her being there, her chatter and her enthusiastic attempts to lay roofing. The memory made him smile. Every time his finger throbbed, Emily's face drifted into his mind. Every time the wind blew the soft fragrance of wildflowers to him, the fragrance he'd smelled in her hair last night, Emily flooded his thoughts.

Giving up, he climbed down from the roof and headed for the house.

In the kitchen, he found a note from Emily. She'd gone shopping and he'd had a phone call from a man named Pritchard.

Kat stared down at the number she'd scrawled in green ink on the corner of a napkin, wondering if this would be the day that would end his search. Carrying the number with him, he went to the wall phone, then dialed. The phone rang.

When he heard a female voice say, "J. R. Pritchard, Associates. May I help you?" Kat let out a breath he'd been unaware he was holding.

He recognized the sultry voice of the secretary with the fake eyelashes. "This is Rian Madison. I have a message here to call Mr. Pritchard."

"Yes, Mr. Madison, if you'll hold, I'll put you through."

While he waited, Kat listened absently to the canned music drifting through the receiver. His gaze wandered to a crack in the kitchen ceiling. He'd have to fix that before it got worse.

"Pritchard here."

"Pritchard. Rian Madison. You have some information for me."

"Right. Let me find your file."

While Pritchard shuffled papers, Kat leaned around the casing of the window and checked the driveway for Emily.

"Here it is," Pritchard said, drawing Kat's attention back to their conversation. "One of my men got some information for you in…" Again a pause, this time Kat suspected Pritchard was scanning the report his employee had turned in. "…Westchester County. Place called Adams Falls. There's a wood-carver who lived there and one of the towns people recalls him carving pieces decorated with that rose you gave me."

One word of Pritchard's report struck him. "Lived? Is he dead?"

"No. But he's been residing in a nursing home for over a year now. From the report I have in front of me, he's been in and out of a coma for the last three weeks and things aren't looking too good, so I'd advise you to talk to him as soon as you can."

"I'm leaving right away."

Kat used the napkin with Emily's message to him to take down the man's name and the address of the nursing home and then hung up. He stared at his scrawl for a few long moments before bolting toward the stairs to shower and change.

EMILY PICKED UP her leather shoulder bag from the car's seat, then slid from the driver's side onto her driveway. The whole shopping trip had been a co-lossal waste of time. Either the nightwear she looked at left her half nude or it covered her from chin to toes. She didn't want to look like a hooker when she went after Kat. Neither did she want to look like a cloistered nun. Something somewhere in between would have been nice.

Sighing half in frustration and half in exhaustion, she glanced around for a sign that Kat was home, but his truck was missing. She listened for sounds of work coming from the house next door. All was quiet.

Tucking her car keys into her purse, she headed up the stairs, then through the front door. She listened for signs that Kat was home. The house remained quiet except for the soft clatter of the loose shutter on the kitchen window. She checked the kitchen table where they'd taken to leaving notes for each other. Again, nothing.

Panic began to seep in around the edges of her concern. For him to leave and not tell her where he'd gone and when he'd be back was very odd. Funny, she'd gotten used to that so easily. So, if he wasn't here, where was he and why hadn't he left a note? Unless—

Quickly, she dropped her purse on the kitchen table and raced up the stairs to the spare room. She knocked quietly and listened. Deafening silence. Hating herself for doubting, but unable to push the uncertainties aside, she swung open the door and stepped inside. She made her way to the closet and opened the door. All his clothes still hung in neat rows on the clothes bar, his suitcase perched on the top shelf, his shoes lined up on the floor, next to a wooden cradle.

Now that she knew he hadn't just vanished again, a strange feeling flooded her. It was more than just relief, she felt secure again, safe.

Her gaze fell on the cradle. A cradle? In Kat's closet? Squatting, she took a closer look.

Obviously handmade of pine and lovingly polished to a high, glossy sheen, it was too big for a doll, but just the right size for a baby. Who did it belong to and who had made it? Kat's father had been a schoolteacher who had had to call a carpenter to glue a chair leg. Turning the cradle into the light to get a better look, she noticed a carving at the end, a heart entwined by a vine bearing roses. She ran her hand over the wood, wondering if this cradle had been Kat's and if one day their child might sleep in it.

Their child. When had she begun to think in terms of the child belonging to both of them? The idea of accepting Kat so totally into her life scared Emily enough to make her push the cradle back into the closet, close the door and scamper from the room.

As she rushed down the stairs, she heard the back door closing. Thinking it was Kat, she hurried into the kitchen to give him a tongue-lashing for not leaving her a note. But when she rounded the door, she came face to face with Bert, her foreman's assistant.

He looked apologetic. "I knocked, but when no one answered, I let myself in. Figured with all these lights on, someone had to be here." His gaze dropped to the toes of his scuffed boots.

She patted his sleeve, still experiencing the wash

of calmness she'd derived from realizing that Kat hadn't left her. "What is it, Bert?"

"It's Midnight Lady." He frowned. "I think she's going into labor."

"But she's not due for another couple of weeks at least."

"She's moving around the stall, won't lay down."

"There could be a million other reasons for that."

Bert shook his head. A wave of gray hair fell over his right eyebrow. "Could be, Miss, but I got a gut feeling that it's more than that."

Emily knew Bert's gut feelings. Chuck put great store in them and so did she. The man seemed to have a connection to every horse on the place, and until someone proved otherwise, both she and Chuck viewed Bert's gut-instinct as a red-light alert.

"Let's take a look. We can't afford to have anything happening to her or her foal. Chuck says her owners will probably bring her back to be bred again, if all goes right this time."

Bert nodded, then stepped aside for her to go out the door ahead of him. Quickly, the two of them hurried toward the foaling barn.

KAT PARKED HIS TRUCK beside Emily's. He ran his fingers through his hair and sighed. A whole day wasted. A trip that had resulted in nothing. He hit the palm of his hand against the steering wheel. Just his luck that the old man had lapsed back into a coma just before he got there. Kat wasn't sure if he was angry or just plain disappointed that he'd hit another dead end. He'd just have to wait for the nursing home to contact him when the old man could talk.

Opening the truck door, he glanced toward the lighted living-room window. At that moment, he realized he'd walked out and never left a note for Emily. The problem of not finding the answers to his question about the identity of his birth parents vanished in the face of what Emily must be thinking. Knowing her penchant for not only jumping to the wrong conclusions, but also for putting the worst spin on things, she'd probably figured he'd run off again. He slammed the truck door. Taking the stairs two at a time, he hurried up the front porch.

Entering the living room and expecting to find Emily curled in her usual spot at the end of the couch, the TV playing softly, he was surprised to find the room empty, the TV dark. He looked toward the kitchen. Again, when he entered the lit room, it was empty, but through the window, he could see lights coming from the foaling barn.

Concern forming a knot of apprehension in his gut, he headed out the back door toward the barn. When he got within several feet of the building, he slowed his stride. He could hear the sound of Emily singing a lullaby. Quietly, he stepped into the barn and walked toward the sound of her voice.

Inside the end stall, Emily was kneeling on the straw-covered floor. In front of her knees a big horse lay quietly while she stroked its muzzle and sang. Each time the horse moved, she dipped her head closer to its ear and sang a little softer. The horse went quiet again.

Kat had seen her do this many times when they were kids. Her compassion for the animal communicated itself through her voice, and the horse became as docile as a kitten, seeming to understand the love she held in her heart for them.

''Problem?'' he asked softly, so as not to frighten either her or the horse. She started anyway. The look of relief in her eyes, when she raised her gaze to his, told him he'd been right to worry about her reaction to him forgetting to leave a note. Her words confirmed it.

''You came back.''

''Of course. Why would you think I wouldn't?''

Not until she heard Kat say the words had she realized the extent of her fear that he'd left again, for good. ''You didn't come back before,'' she reminded him without accusing.

He stepped into the stall and came down beside her. He slipped an arm around her shoulders then pulled her to him. ''I promised I would be here and I will. I'm sorry, if I frightened you. I will never walk out again and not tell you where I'm going or when I'll be back.''

Grateful for the words she knew were offered to dispel her fear of him leaving, Emily couldn't believe him, no matter how much she longed to. He'd promised before and broken his promise, and she just couldn't risk more damage to her heart by believing that he wouldn't do it again.

He touched the side of the horse's head with his palm. "What's wrong?"

"The foal has a leg twisted beneath him. Bert's gone for the vet." As another contraction hit her, Midnight Lady whinnied loudly. She tried to raise her head. With Kat's help, Emily pressed it back down. She began humming softly again and petting the dark golden muzzle with long, slow strokes. "The poor thing is terrified. This is her first."

Kat stood, then walked to the back of the horse. He returned to Emily's side, then squatted down, his brows drawn together in concern. "One hoof is starting to show. Can you hold her head?"

Emily nodded. "Why? What are you going to do?"

Kat stood, pulled his shirt from his pants, then began unbuttoning it. "Unfold that leg before the hoof tears her uterus apart." He stood back and looked down at her and the horse. "She been in labor for a while?" Emily nodded. "If we let her go, she won't be strong enough to help with the birth. But the fact that she's not terribly strong might be helpful. I won't have to worry too much about being hit by a flying hoof."

Emily hadn't thought about the danger Kat was putting himself in. One blow from Lady's hoof and he could well get killed or seriously injured. She reached for his hand. He paused, a question in his gaze.

"Maybe we should wait for the vet."

He squatted beside her and held her hand in his.

Raising it, he kissed the back of her fingers. "I am a vet, Em. Got my degree about eight years ago."

Eight years? And she never knew? He never offered to tell her? It hit home suddenly just how very far apart they'd grown. The realization brought pain and a feeling of isolation she had trouble explaining.

He started to move away again. Impulsively, she grabbed for his hand and wrapped her fingers tightly around it. "Be careful."

For a long moment, he studied her. She could feel emotions rising up in her and threatening to overflow, emotions that left her weak and frightened of their consequences. "I need you."

His face crumbled, as if she'd hurt him. "How could I forget?" He abruptly dropped her hand and moved out of her line of vision. "Since she's about ready to finish the job she's started, this shouldn't take too long, but I'm going to have to push her baby back into the birth canal far enough so I can unfold that leg. She's going to object to this, so hold onto her head. Okay?"

"Yes." Emily clamped her arms around Lady's neck and threw her body forward, hoping her added weight would be enough to hold the mare's head down.

"Ready?"

She tightened her hold until her arms started to ache. "Ready."

Emily knew the exact moment when Kat inserted his arm into the birth canal. Lady flinched, straining against Emily's hold, but she kept the horse's head pressed against the floor. Her shoulders ached and her muscles felt like they were on fire, but she held on, knowing if the horse threw out her legs and tried to stand, Kat might get hit. Again Lady pushed against Emily. Again she held fast and hummed into Lady's ear. Lady quieted. She never took her gaze off the horse. The wet sound of Kat's quest to unfold the leg was the only indication she had that anything was happening behind her.

When it seemed like hours had passed and she was sure she could hold on no longer, Lady's nostrils flared, her eyes grew big and her sides gave a mighty heave.

Kat's voice broke the silence. "It's a boy!"

While Lady forced herself to her feet, Emily rolled free. Kat cleaned the membrane from the foal's head, then stood aside while Lady expelled the placenta. He patted her neck, then stepped outside the stall.

Moving to Kat's side, Emily got her first glimpse of the wet, spindly-legged, miniature horse, wobbling and fighting to stand up. Lady licked his body and nuzzled him with her nose, trying to assist the foal to his feet. As they got acquainted, Emily stared intently at the momma and baby.

"Beautiful isn't it?" Kat's voice came from close by her ear.

"Yes. It never ceases to amaze me." But Emily knew that this birth hit her even harder in the heart than all the others she'd watched. This time, it reminded her of the baby she longed for—Kat's baby. She thought about the empty cradle in his closet and hoped their baby would have a chance to occupy it.

Down deep, something told her that it *was* Kat's and that he had a strong attachment to it. Why, she wasn't sure, but it seemed only right that one day his child should sleep there.

Suddenly, so many emotions accosted her at once that she found herself fighting back tears. She wanted that baby, but, God help her, she also wanted Kat.

The time had come for her to stop fooling herself about this business arrangement and to admit that it was more than that. How much more she wasn't sure. But tonight she'd find out. She turned to Kat. Her breath caught in her chest.

Bent over the sink at the other side of the barn, Kat splashed water on himself, washing the evidence of the birth off his arms and upper torso. Highlighted by the glow from the dim bulb hanging from the ceiling, the muscles in his back bunched and relaxed with his every movement. Dots of moisture sparkled on his deeply tanned skin. His dark hair brushed his shoulders. His jeans rode low on his slim hips, making her wish they'd—

He turned toward her. His gaze met hers. Emily swallowed hard.

Like a stalked animal, he stood very still, as if assessing his adversary. The towel he'd been drying himself with dropped from his fingers. Slowly, he walked toward her. The straw crunched softly beneath his boots. He stopped close enough for her to feel the gentle brush of his breath on her warm cheeks, the heat from his body joining hers.

As if drawn by some invisible magnet, her attention shifted to the stack of blankets she'd brought to the barn earlier, expecting a long night's vigil.

He followed her glance, then returned his gaze to hers. "Is this it, Em? Are you asking?"

Insanely, she recalled her exhausting search for the sexy nighty. Ironically, now that *the moment* had arrived, clothing didn't seem to matter so much any more.

Chapter Eight

The barn had become hazy. Dreamlike. There, but not there. Emily's gaze, captured by the dark pools of Kat's eyes, never shifted, even when the new foal whinnied plaintively in the stall behind her. She waited for Kat's next move. Her blood pumped through her veins at an alarming rate, echoing in her ears like a sensual drumbeat. Warmth unlike any she'd experienced suffused her body.

Hay rustled beneath her shifting feet, the clean smell of its freshness surrounding them. She'd envisioned their first time taking place amid the fragrance of the expensive perfume Jess had sent her for her birthday. But, at this instant, perfume didn't matter any more than the sexy nightgown. The man looking at her with desire in his eyes had canceled all that out.

Certain that she couldn't, she waited, hoping he'd close the gap separating them. Not that she didn't want to take that last step, the step that would put her in his arms, but she couldn't get her body to obey, nor could she get her vocal cords to convey her wishes.

But Kat stood his ground. "You have to come to me, Em. You have to make the first move."

In the end, desire for him, not any conscious effort on her part, drove her into his embrace.

His arms closed around her. She rested her cheek against his bare skin and fought for her next breath. She'd come home. The smell of him, the feel of his skin, the beat of his heart combined to send her senses into a tailspin. Lord, but she wanted this man and no amount of denying it was going to change that.

Kat hooked his finger under her chin and raised her face. He looked into her eyes, and, as if reading what he saw there, he smiled. His head lowered slowly. His breath brushed her sensitive skin. He pulled her closer, shaping her body to his.

Then his lips touched hers, gently at first, then harder, more demanding. Heat waves washed over her. She tightened her arms, pulling his mouth even closer. When he gently pried at her lips, she opened them and received him eagerly. Vaguely, she wondered if she'd feel the same with any man who kissed her. Instantly, she knew she wouldn't. Kat was special, special in her mind and in her heart. He always had been and always would be.

When he moved his hand from her back and slid it around her rib cage, she sucked in her breath. Her body stiffened, waiting for the touch of his hand on her breast. He separated their lips just far enough to be able to speak.

"Easy, Em. Relax. Follow me. Let me love you."

His words gentled her, much as she had gentled Lady. Her body slumped against him, her legs no longer strong enough to hold her. As she always had, she relied on Kat's strength to support her. Very slowly, he moved his hand and engulfed her breast.

Sparks of fire raced up and down her body. This was what she'd been waiting for, longing for since their first kiss. Why had she put it off? Why had she been afraid to let go? Why was it still not enough, not nearly enough?

For a very long moment, Kat remained still, as if allowing her to get used to the sensations bombarding her. Then he moved his fingers, massaging, caressing, sweeping her into a world of sensations and emotions swamping her body and her mind. He dipped his hand and slid it beneath the hem of her shirt.

Bare skin on bare skin. Emily was certain she'd either collapse at his feet, nerveless and boneless, at his mercy, or she'd come apart from all that she was feeling. Neither happened. Instead, she weathered the newest wave of passion overwhelming her and closed her mind to thought. She wanted only to feel, to savor what Kat was doing to her. To savor Kat— her friend, her husband and soon, her lover.

Kat had imagined what it would be like to hold Emily, to make love to her, but nothing he could have imagined came close to the real thing. It shouldn't have, but her open response to him and her naked passion surprised him. Em did everything with unbridled passion. It followed that she'd make love with just as much intensity. It seemed he'd waited a lifetime for this moment. Maybe he had. Maybe it had always been Emily.

She whimpered and settled closer to him, running her hands over his back, digging her nails into his flesh. Such sweet pain. Need gouged a pathway through him, furrowing deep into his body. He wanted Emily as he'd never wanted any woman. He needed her as he'd never needed any woman.

He guided her toward the pile of blankets in the corner of the barn. Never taking his hand from her breast, relishing the feel of her smooth skin. Basking in the heat of her body and the small sounds she made each time he moved his hand against her.

"In here, Doc."

The voice of Emily's assistant foreman hit Kat like a winter rain. He sprang back from her, leaving her to stare at him with glazed eyes. Quickly, he pulled her shirt down and straightened her clothes, then stepped in front of her, giving her time to gather her wits.

Bert entered the barn, followed closely by an older man carrying a small brown leather bag. "Kat, this here's Doc Grayson."

Nodding, Kat recognized the vet immediately and remained in the shadows, hoping the old man would not recognize him and perpetuate explanations he wasn't ready to give just yet. "Sir."

The foreman glanced around. "Where's Miss Emily?"

"I'm here, Bert." Emily came around Kat looking remarkably recovered. She never looked at him, just walked straight to the vet and shook his hand. "Thanks for coming, but I'm afraid it's all over but the shouting. Lady didn't want to wait, so Kat helped me deliver the foal. He's an old friend, but he's also a vet." Her voice wavered only slightly, not enough for anyone but Kat to notice.

Left with no choice, Kat stepped into the dim light of the barn and extended his hand.

Doc Grayson shook the hand Kat offered, then studied him. "Don't we know each other, son?"

Kat squirmed. He'd hoped he'd changed enough that his old professor wouldn't remember him. "Yes, sir. Rian Madison. You taught a couple of the classes I took when I was at Cornell getting my degree." He avoided looking at Emily, but he heard the tiny gasp of surprise that followed his words.

Grayson dropped his bag. "Sure, I remember now. *Kat* threw me. You were one of my best students. I wasn't at Cornell too long. Left the year you graduated. Hated not working with the animals. Guess I wasn't meant to be a teacher." He grinned. "Let's have a look at the mare and the little one, not that I don't think you did your job right, son."

Kat followed the vet into the stall without a backward glance at Emily. She stared after them. Cornell? That was just north of here. Kat had been so close, for all that time, and never come home to see her, never let her know? The realization hurt.

Knowing the mare and the foal were in good hands and unable to face Kat without spitting out her anger at his deliberate abandonment when she'd needed a friend so desperately, she left the shed. Her mind whirled with the old pain of their severed friendship, the residue of their encounter and a realization she could no longer deny. She had fallen hopelessly in love with Kat Madison.

Fallen was the right word all right. She'd stumbled blindly into a situation that would put not only her peace of mind at risk, but also her heart. The worst of it was, through her own edict that she'd expect him to leave once the baby was conceived, she'd made his eventual departure a foregone conclusion.

EMILY HEARD KAT come up the stairs an hour later, then pause outside her room. She held her breath, hoping he would not come in. She wasn't ready to face him yet, mostly because of the encounter in the barn, but partly because of his deception.

How could he have been so close and not come to see her? Why had he done it? Somewhere inside herself, she knew it had something to do with this secret he kept from her, the secret he'd promised to reveal when the time was right. Until she knew the details, did she have the right to hold it against him? No, she didn't. He might have had a good reason for staying away. She'd have to wait until he was ready to fill in the sixteen years they'd been apart.

She sat on the edge of her bed and stared out the window into the star-filled sky. Her thoughts darted back to the scene in the barn after the foal's birth. She could still feel Kat's hands against her skin, and the sensations awakened by his touch gnawed at her insides, like a starving beast waiting to be appeased.

Dare she go to him, in hopes that they could continue what they'd started? Dare she risk her heart to a man who had come back into her life as easily as he had walked out? Did she have a choice? Loving him narrowed down the field. He'd obviously wanted her as much as she'd wanted him.

Resolutely, before she could second-guess herself and allow those insidious doubts to creep into her mind, she stood and went to her dresser. From the second drawer, she extracted one of her newest flannel nightgowns, a white background with tiny yellow carnations scattered all over it. She held it in front of her and looked at her reflection. Wrinkling her nose, she opened her manicure case and took out a small pair of cuticle scissors.

Laying the gown flat on the bed, she began to cut away the sleeves, plunge the neckline and remove what she felt was the right amount of skirt-length to achieve her goal of sexy. When she'd finished, she rubbed at the sore spots on her fingers caused by forcing the tiny scissors through two layers of thick flannel.

Holding the gown up to herself again, she smiled at her reflection. Removing her clothes, she took a quick shower, blew her hair dry and donned the redesigned gown. To her utter shock, she'd hacked off a lot more of the skirt than she'd intended, leaving certain body parts she'd rather not have exposed in plain view.

Once more she dived into her drawer. This time,

she extracted a pair of sheer, pale yellow bikini panties. After putting them on, she surveyed herself again. Perfect.

Ready to walk out the door, she hesitated. Suppose Kat didn't think she looked sexy? It would just kill the mood. She grabbed her old green chenille robe from the foot of the bed and slipped into it.

In the hall, her courage began to wane, but she forced herself to keep going until she stood outside Kat's bedroom door. Carefully, she opened it and stepped inside. Kat lay unmoving, the sheets draped across his waist, his hair damp from his shower, one strong hand curled next to his face on the pillow. A shaft of moonlight fell across his cheek.

Her breath caught. The handsome teenaged Kat that the girls had chased relentlessly couldn't hold a candle to the devastating man he'd become. Did women still chase after him? The thought brought the acrid taste of jealousy rising in her throat.

She stripped her mind of all thought except making love with this man who was her husband. Emily slipped closer to the big oak-framed bed.

How would Rose accept this addition to their household? For so many years it had been just Emily and Rose occupying this big house, depending on each other for everything. Now, Kat was here. Thankfully, Emily still had time to prepare her old friend for the addition to their household before she came home. She'd call Rose in the morning.

She moved closer. A board creaked in protest at her weight.

Kat stirred. Sucking in her breath, Emily paused.

This was absurd. Why was she trying not to wake him when that's exactly what she'd come here to do? His breathing settled back to normal; she moved to the side of the bed.

"Kat?"

Nothing.

Tentatively, she touched his arm. "Kat?" He remained motionless. "Are you dead?"

No, not dead, Kat reassured her silently, *just waiting to see what you're going to do, how far you'll go.* After what she'd learned about him in the barn, he'd expected her to give him the cold shoulder for a week. When his door had swung open and she'd stepped in, it had surprised him. He lifted an eyelid to a slit opening.

Emily stood close enough for him to touch. She was busy slipping her robe from her shoulders. He nearly sucked in an audible breath at the brief nightgown she wore. Lord, but the woman knew exactly how to tantalize a man and stir his desires.

"Kat, are you awake?" She sat down on the side of the bed and touched his bare arm again.

Shock waves scooted across his skin. He had to fight himself to lie still and wait.

"Kat?" She shook him very gently, and when he didn't respond, she sighed and started to stand.

Afraid that she'd leave, he snared her wrist and dragged her down across him on the bed.

"You were awake all the time," she accused, glaring down at him from where she lay sprawled across his chest.

"Guilty."

"Why?"

"I was waiting to see what nefarious means you'd use to seduce me."

She sat up and stuck out her chin indignantly. "I was *not* trying to seduce you, just wake you up."

"Oh? And do you always dress so sexily to wake up your houseguests?"

Her expression became indignant. "I'm not… no…that is…" When she realized he wasn't buying it, her indignation faded. She reached for her robe.

Kat grabbed her hand. "No. Don't cover up. You're very lovely. Be proud of who you are, what you are." He removed the robe from her fingers and dropped it to the floor.

She dipped her head and began rolling the raw edge of flannel at the hem of the nightgown, or what was left of it. "I'm embarrassed."

"Why? You have nothing to be embarrassed about." She still avoided his gaze. "Look at me." He hooked her chin and raised her gaze to his. "Em, it's okay. I'm sorry I teased you. You can seduce me all you want. I promise I won't fight." He smiled.

When she returned his smile, he knew he'd gotten through to her. "Why don't you just climb in here with me and we'll talk." She hesitated. "Just talk." He held up his fingers in a version of the Boy Scouts' salute. "Scout's honor."

She stood, turned, then slipped into the bed beside him. Hugging her side of the large bed, she lay perfectly still, staring at the dark ceiling. Kat chuckled, then looped his arm around her and drew her to him, settling her head against his shoulder.

"Kat?" She snuggled down against him, placing her leg over his, seemingly unperturbed by his state of complete undress. Would the woman ever stop surprising him?

He swallowed hard. "Hm." He had to concentrate on something besides the way her hair smelled and how soft her skin felt on his and the way her curves seemed to nestle perfectly into the contours of his body, as if she'd been made especially for him to hold.

"Why didn't you come to see me while you were at Cornell?"

Hell and damnation! He'd hoped she'd forgotten about that. "I though it best to stay away."

Emily raised her head to look at him. "Does it have anything to do with...with that thing you said you'd tell me about later?"

"Yes."

She stared at him for a moment, then lay back down and snuggled into the crook of his arm, raising his blood pressure another several hundred degrees. "Okay. I can wait."

"Em?"

"Yes?"

"Thanks for trusting me on that. It means a lot. I will talk to you about it, but when the time is right."

She propped herself up on one elbow, then ran the backs of her fingers over his cheek. "I know."

Did that mean she was learning to trust him? He

hoped so. Em had so little trust for any man. That she found it difficult to trust came as no great revelation to him. After living with Frank Kingston and his broken promises, it was a wonder she trusted anyone to keep their word to her.

"Kat?"

"Yes."

"Will you…uh…kiss me the way you did in the barn?" She'd tilted her head so that the moonlight fell across her face, illuminating the contours of her cheeks and lips.

Without saying a word, because he was too filled with emotion to speak, Kat leaned forward and gently laid his lips on hers. What started out as a sweet kiss, filled with tenderness and hesitation, soon gathered heat. Before he knew what was happening, Emily had looped her arms around his neck and pulled him down into an all-out, soul-searching, flaming kiss that rocked his foundation and turned his body to a torch.

Emily could fight her hunger for Kat no longer. When he finally kissed her and made no move to deepen the kiss, she did it for him. However, rather than appeasing her hunger, the kiss inflamed her more. She wanted—no, needed more. She needed him.

Kat pulled back, leaving her clutching at him. "Em, are you sure? If you aren't, stop me now, because soon I won't be able to stop."

She stared up at him, allowing him to see the passion she knew must be written clearly in her eyes. "Don't stop."

A deep sigh of contentment issued from Kat. This was what he'd been dreaming of for days, making love to Emily. He wasn't sure where it would lead, and right now he didn't care. All he could think of was Emily, being beside her, inside her, loving her, being loved by her.

He eased his hand down her side to cup her breast. Tenderly, he kneaded her flesh, listening to the soft moans of pleasure issuing from her. God, what that did for a man, to know he could please his woman. His woman. Yes, Emily was definitely his woman and more. Emily was the woman he loved, the woman he wanted to have at his side in old age, the woman who had gone from friend to lover in a few short days.

Slowly, he slid her nightgown from her shoulders, covering the exposed flesh with hot kisses, making his mark. She moved restlessly against him, grinding her body into his.

With swift movements, he pulled the gown over her head, then slipped the panties down her hips and off her feet. She lay before him, naked, lovely, intoxicating. He held his breath, frightened that she'd bolt or that she'd disappear and he'd find he'd been dreaming. But then she rolled toward him, pressing her nakedness the length of him and he knew this was no dream. If it was, he prayed never to awaken.

Emily was shocked by her own aggressiveness. She wanted to touch him, to have him touch her, to feel his response to her. For the first time in her life she really felt like a woman and she loved it. She loved him. She opened her mouth to tell him, but he covered it with his, prying her lips apart, exploring the depths with his tongue. He emulated the movements of love with his tongue and her mind reeled with desire.

Kat kissed her long and deep, then slipped over her. She opened to him, eager for their joining, wanting him as close and as much a part of her as possible. Only for a second did she regret that she could not give him the gift of being first. Then he was inside her and all thought meshed with sensation.

She held her breath at the joy that arced through her, the contentment, the love. At last, she and Kat were really one, more than their vows had made them, more than heaven and earth could make them. One as a single entity striving toward the same glorious conclusion.

The end came in a burst of light and sensation too overwhelming for Emily to stand. She cried out his name and clutched at him, wanting it never to end, to keep him forever in her arms.

But end it did, and only then did Emily realize she'd never given one thought to this act of love being a prelude to the child they had agreed to parent. It had been for her and Kat. If a child had been conceived as a result, then that would be the most marvelous gift she could think of, but for now, this moment was hers and Kat's alone. Something to tuck into her memory and never let go. Something to have of him when he was gone again.

Content, she nestled next to him, his arms around

her, his lips against her hair and allowed sleep to overcome her.

Kat had never felt so complete in his life. Even with the missing parts of his childhood, he still relished the feeling of wholeness Emily had given him. He pulled her closer, wanting to hold her for the rest of his days, but knowing she didn't want that. Some of the brilliance of their moments together faded. Could he make her see this was what true happiness was? Could he make Emily truly his, forever?

SUNLIGHT SLANTED across Emily's face where it rested on Kat's bare chest. She blinked and tried to bring her surroundings into focus. Her abused muscles reminded her of the night before and the intense passion they'd shared. Had that passion-inflamed woman really been her?

She glanced at Kat, still sleeping, traced his bottom lip with the tip of her finger, then, when he wrinkled his nose and turned his face away from the annoyance disturbing his deep sleep, she smiled. Love swelled inside her. Along with it came a deep, gnawing ache. How would she ever let him go again?

Her romantic musings were abruptly interrupted by a startled gasp from the direction of the door. Yanking the sheet up to cover her nakedness and Kat's face, Emily turned to confront the intruder.

In the doorway, mouth agape, eyes large, her cheeks red with embarrassment, stood Rose.

Chapter Nine

"Now, what am I going to do?" Emily stood over Kat, a vision of Rose's shocked expression still fresh in her mind. He lay beneath the sheets on the rumpled bed watching her frantic pacing with a smile of questionable nature curving his lips. "You could at least have said something."

"And exactly what was it I should have said? When you so cleverly hid me beneath the sheet, I was under the impression you'd rather I kept my mouth shut."

Emily paused long enough to throw him an impatient glare. "That was an accident." On her return trip past the bed, she stopped again and glared at him. "Hells bells, Kat. We were both naked. What would you have had me do, invite her to join us?"

A chuckle rumbled through his wide chest. "And me playing ostrich with a sheet over my head was your answer?"

She made a face at him. " I told you that was an accident. And you might stop being sarcastic and help."

"For starters, *you* might have tried telling her that we're married and that you haven't sold yourself into prostitution. I'll bet she's downstairs imagining all kinds of scenarios."

Men! They had no sense of timing. Even if he was right, and he probably was, and Rose was downstairs imagining the worst, she couldn't just blurt something like that out. Not being told about the wedding before it happened would hurt Rose. Any explanation had to be approached with finesse. And right now, she didn't have a clue as to how to face the woman waiting in the kitchen for that explanation.

"Hey, Squirt." She looked at him. He quirked his finger. "Come here." Patting the side of the bed, he shifted to make room for her.

The sheet covering the lower half of his torso slipped a couple of inches, threatening to reveal what lay below its snowy white folds. Emily jerked the tie of her robe tighter and inhaled sharply. "I'll stay right where I am, thank you very much."

The last thing she needed right now was another romp in the hay with Kat, even though, way back in her mind, the thought presented some interesting possibilities.

She halted her thoughts short of examining those possibilities. Bad enough that last night still played in her head like an NFL instant replay and that her skin still tingled every time she thought of making love with Kat. Thoughts like that would only pave the way for more problems and right now she had enough to think about. She wouldn't be in this mess if she'd stop letting her emotions overrule her common sense.

Now that the flames from the night before had died down, she had some serious questions running around in her head about her feelings for Kat and what exactly she'd be left with, once the child had been conceived.

Just the fact that the baby had never entered her mind the night before scared the bejesus out of her. What had happened in this bed had not been to save her home, as she'd intended in the beginning, but had carried some much deeper meaning, a meaning she refused to consider right now. Later. She'd think about it later.

First, she had to take care of the situation with Rose. She wasn't sure if Rose's red cheeks had indicated embarrassment or anger. Knowing Rose, it could be one or both of the above. If Kat could put his carnal thoughts on hold, she might find a solution to going downstairs and facing her surrogate mother. But were *his* carnal thoughts really the problem? She glanced at him.

He raised one eyebrow and grinned that heart-stopping smile that grabbed her heart and turned it to mush.

Oh damn!

"Scared to venture too close to the wolf's lair?"

"No. Why should I be scared? I spent the night here with you, or has that slipped your mind?"

Slipped his mind? Fat chance. He recalled every minute detail with vivid clarity. And while spending another hour or two with Emily in the big bed was very tempting, his main concern at the moment was erasing the worry lines from her forehead and helping her face Rose.

"Em, come sit here." He patted the bed and waited.

"You promise to just talk? Nothing more?"

He raised his hand. "Promise."

She stepped around the footboard, then took a seat at the foot of the bed, far enough away, he noted, that he couldn't reach her, and if he tried, easy to make a getaway.

"Okay. I'm here. Now what?" She toyed with end of one of the frayed ties on her bathrobe, knotting it and unknotting it.

"We'll go down together and tell her that we got married. Period. Anything beyond that is our business and no one else's."

She stared at him, her eyes large moist pools of worry. "I can't do that. I've never kept secrets from Rose."

"Do you want her to know that our marriage is for convenience only and that as soon as we conceive a child, we'll be heading for a lawyer's office? Would that be easier to explain to her?" Kat hated the subterfuge as much as he knew Emily did, but to tell her friend, whom she obviously loved, that their marriage was a sham, would cause more harm than good at this point. "You can tell her the whole story after I'm gone."

The words cut deep into his soul. But until Emily made it clear that she wanted him around for the duration, if she ever did, he had to think that way or go crazy with what-ifs and maybes. He'd had enough uncertainties and unanswered questions in his life already. No sense deliberately adding to his list.

She dipped her head, hiding her expression from him, so he had no way of knowing how she'd received his last statement. If last night indicated how she felt, he had an inkling that she just might be experiencing more than friendship for her old playmate. However, from his experience, women could have just as good a time in the sack as men without forging any emotional bonds. So, until he knew for certain, he was not about to lay his heart on the chopping block.

"Em, are you ready to go downstairs?"

A long moment passed before she looked up, then nodded. "I guess so." She offered him a watery smile. "Our only other alternative would be to climb out my bedroom window and down the maple tree, like we did when I was ten to escape my father's wrath."

"And we got caught, if you recall."

"And you took the full blame." She smiled at him, defusing some of the tension.

He shrugged, encouraging the conversation, hoping it would help relax her. "It wasn't bad. *Someone* had to clean up the cow. And I did paint most of the roses on it." The recollection made them both smile. "It only took a few days to get the paint off."

The same devilish smile she'd had all those years

ago flashed across Emily's face. "You have to admit, she was unique when we'd finished decorating her." Emily began to laugh again and he joined in.

The sound filled the room—and Kat. He loved to see her laugh. He loved to see her happy. He loved her. As if on cue, the laughter faded and their gazes locked.

"Kat, I never really said thank you for all the times you were there for me, at least until…" She turned away.

He didn't have to ask to know what she was thinking. That when she needed him most, he hadn't been there.

He sat up and then slid near enough to scoop her to him. With her head nestled into his neck and his arms around her, he whispered into her hair. "I'll be with you. From now on, for as long as you want me, I'll be with you."

For as long as *she* wanted *him*. What about him? Did he want to stay? Dare she ask?

Though she tried to believe his sincerity, she still couldn't. She hated that she relied on him to help her through this explanation to Rose. She hated that he had helped her last night with the foal. She hated that he had become such a necessary part of her life again. Because one day, she knew he'd leave, no matter how many promises he made to the contrary. Because, the bottom line was that staying with her wasn't what he wanted.

Frank Kingston's words whispered through her mind. *Promises are made to be broken, little girl.*

EMILY WATCHED ROSE go about the process of preparing French toast. Her tension eased. French toast was Emily's favorite breakfast and Rose's peacemaker. Whenever she and Rose had had a falling-out in the past, French toast had always bridged the gap and healed the riff. Emily hoped it still would.

Her one saving grace was that Rose didn't seem mad. Maybe, when Rose had discovered them upstairs in the bed, she hadn't been as mad as she had looked. Maybe this wouldn't be as difficult as Emily had first imagined.

She glanced at Kat. He'd been watching her watch Rose. He reached across the table and squeezed her hand, then winked. She pulled her hand back, determined to do this without his help. After all, she'd have to learn not to rely on him soon enough. What better time to start than now?

Rose, who'd been systematically ignoring Emily and Kat since they'd entered the kitchen, placed the egg-saturated bread on the griddle. The smell of the cinnamon she sprinkled over each slice filled the kitchen. The sound of it cooking joined that of the bacon sizzling in the frying pan next to it. As Emily chose her words of explanation, she counted the drops of moisture racing down the side of her orange-juice glass to puddle on the blue vinyl tablecloth. "Rose, I—"

"Emily Kingston," Rose interrupted, her back to them, her gaze centered on the cooking bread, "when I took over here as housekeeper, I promised your daddy that I'd look after you. God knows, you're a grown woman, with a mind of your own.

I have no right telling you how to run your life, but I'm disappointed.''

"Disappointed?" Emily looked from Rose's stiff back to Kat, who shrugged.

"Disappointed that you'd go against everything I taught you about a woman saving herself for the right man. Disappointed that you'd bring this into this house.''

"But—''

Rose swung around. Hurt, rather than anger, showed on her face. "No buts to it, young lady. Acting recklessly can only lead to trouble. Big trouble. This kind of thoughtless, selfish behavior ruins lives. It severs families. It—'' Her voice choked off. She wiped impatiently at the tears streaming down her face.

Stunned by the force of Rose's words and alarmed by her tears, Emily could only stare. She wanted to go to Rose, but before she could motivate her body, Kat got up and went to stand beside Rose. "Rose, Em and I were married almost a week ago.''

Rose looked at Em for confirmation. Em nodded and offered a weak smile. Suddenly, Rose raised her hands to the ceiling and grinned, then rushing to her side, swept Emily into her ample embrace. "Why didn't you tell me, child? I would have flown right home to be with you.'' Then she stiffened and stepped back far enough to look straight into Emily's eyes. "You aren't...''

Emily ignored Kat's speculative expression. "No. I'm not pregnant, Rose.'' At least she didn't think she was. After last night, with any luck, the truth of that statement could come into question, but for now, it remained the truth. "Just happily married."

Rose turned to Kat. "And when do I get an introduction to the new man in my baby's life?"

He stepped forward, glad that these two women had settled things. "I'm not so new. I'm Rian Madison. I lived—"

Rose's face paled and she swayed toward him. Instinctively, he reached for her, catching her just as her legs seemed to crumble beneath her.

"Rose!" Emily took one of Rose's arms and helped Kat guide her to the nearest chair. "I'll get her some water."

Offering them a weak smile, Rose rubbed her forehead. "I'm sorry. I'm all right, really. Just a touch light-headed. Must be the change in climate."

From her pale coloring and the way her voice quivered, Kat had to doubt that. He took the glass of water from Emily and gave it to her housekeeper. "Drink this and sit here for a while."

"But breakfast—"

"I'll finish breakfast." Kat left Rose in Emily's care and went to the stove. After checking on the cooking food, he leaned a hip against the counter and watched the two women.

Rose sent him a doubtful look. "Young man, if you ruin my breakfast, we'll not be off to a good start, you and I."

"He's a great cook," Emily assured, patting Rose's shoulder. "He's the one who kept me alive while you were gone."

"Ah ha, the truth finally comes out." Kat tried not to look too triumphant.

Relaxing after Emily's reassurance that he could handle a spatula with the best, Rose studied him for a moment before leaning back in the chair and centering a loving gaze on Emily.

"Are you sure you're okay?" Emily brushed a strand of brown hair sprinkled with gray from Rose's forehead.

After flipping the French toast and turning the bacon, Kat glanced back to them. Love shone from their faces. This was a lot more than a working relationship. A blind man could see they shared a rare closeness, even if they didn't share the same blood.

"I'm fine, dear. I must have caught a touch of Montezuma's revenge myself," Rose said, her voice sounding a bit stronger. "Poor Helen got it first, and Carol and I made certain not to drink the water and join her, but Carol loves to chew on ice cubes, when the weather is hot. Next thing we knew, she was camped out on her knees with Helen next to the commode." She paused to take a sip of water. "Right then, we decided we might as well come home. Helen and Carol agreed. They said if they were going to spend the next few days worshiping the porcelain god, it might as well be in the comfort and privacy of their own bathrooms." She paused and smiled at them. "Listen to me babbling on."

"I'm sorry your vacation was ruined." Emily squeezed Rose's plump fingers.

Rose had been staring at Kat. "Not to worry. There's always another year." She rose from the chair and shuffled across the floor in a pair of worn pink house slippers to where Kat was transferring the toast to three plates.

The blue-checked curtains, stirred by a soft, cool breeze that brought the smell of freshly cut grass with it, stood out from the open window. The smell mixed with the faint odor of lily of the valley. A wave of contentment washed over him. His adoptive mother had used the same fragrance.

"That's my job," she said taking the spatula from his hand and allowing her palm to brush his for just a second. "You sit down."

He looked at her, about to protest that she should sit for a while longer. Something in her eyes stopped him.

"Please, let me serve you...and Emily your first breakfast as a married couple."

"I'm afraid you're a little late on that score," he joked.

"No. This *is* a first—for me anyway. Please."

Realizing how important this was to Rose, Kat relinquished the spatula and took his seat at the table. He glanced at Emily.

"I think she's forgiven us," she whispered.

"It would seem so."

EMILY DRIED the last of the blue cornflower dinnerware and placed it in the cabinet, then closed the door and put her wet towel over the oven-door handle to dry. She turned to Rose, who was busy wiping off the counter around the sink.

"So, do you like him?" Emily fingered the small gold key at her throat.

Rose continued with her task. Only a slight hesitation in her movements told Emily Rose had even heard her. "It's a little early for a decision, since I hardly know him." She smiled, then ducked her head and went back to wiping the counter. "But anyone who's that handsome and can cook too can't be all bad."

Emily laughed. Knowing that Rose forgave her for not telling her about the marriage, and that she was willing to give Kat a chance spun a warm ring around Emily's heart. Still, there was something about Rose's reserved attitude that disturbed her.

She shrugged it off. Being from the show-me school, it would not be unusual for Rose to hold off on her assessment of Kat until after she got to know him better. And Emily had no doubt that once her old friend did get to know him she'd love him. Kat was that kind of person. Easy to love. Too easy to love.

"I'm sorry we didn't wait until you came home to get married."

Rose dropped her sponge and came to hug Emily to her. "I wish I'd been here. It would be a lie if I said otherwise. But you've given me a great gift, sweet Emily, a precious gift."

"A gift? I don't understand."

Rose pulled back, tears glistening in her blue eyes. She smiled brightly. "For the last sixteen years, I've had two daughters to care for and now...now, I have a son, too. That's a lot for a woman who gave up all hope of having a family years ago.'' A large tear rolled freely down her cheek. She laughed and swiped at it with the corner of her pristine white apron. ''I'm being foolish. Maybe I didn't totally escape Montezuma's revenge after all.''

She moved away from Emily, almost as if trying to hide her joy. Emily followed her, hugged her shoulders from behind, then kissed her cheek. ''Why don't you go lie down for a while. The house will keep.''

''I just might do that.''

Expecting an argument from her friend, Emily tamped down her surprise, lest Rose change her mind. ''Good. I have to check the new foal. I'll be back in time for lunch and you can tell me all about Mexico. Oh, I'll bring Kat with me. If he's not reminded, he works right through meals.''

''Kat?''

''Yes, it's a nickname his parents gave him years ago. He always had this uncanny ability to get into and out of a room without making a noise.'' Emily hurried toward the back door, anxious to see how the newest member of the farm was faring. ''See you later.'' When Rose didn't answer, Emily glanced back over her shoulder. Rose stared out the kitchen window toward the old Madison house, obviously lost in thought.

Chapter Ten

Emily entered the kitchen, then stood beside the refrigerator, her hand resting on the wall telephone receiver. She'd been consciously putting this off for days, and she couldn't put it off any longer.

"Are we expecting an earthquake? I hear telephones just jump right off the wall, if you're not careful." Rose's amused voice came from the other side of the kitchen.

Having thought she was alone, Emily started, then glanced in the direction of the woman snapping green beans into a large, aluminum colander. The last thing she needed right now was Rose as an audience. Emily didn't want to have to get into explaining again why she hadn't called her housekeeper to tell her about the wedding or why she hadn't told her brother yet.

"I'm gathering my thoughts."

"For what? A simple phone call? Who could you be calling that requires all this preparation?"

Emily sighed. Oh well, in for a dime, in for a dollar. "Jesse. When you mentioned him at lunch, it occurred to me that I had never told him about Kat and me getting married."

"It *occurred* to you…. Emily Kings…Madison." Rose frowned and clucked her tongue. "How could you not tell your own brother that you got married?" She wielded a long green bean like an avenging sword, punctuating each word with a stab at the air.

Leaving the phone, happy for an excuse to put off the call for a few more minutes, but not thrilled about having to explain it to Rose first, Emily joined Rose at the table. "Jess was never really interested in what happens here, so I guess I felt he wouldn't be interested in that either." She absently picked up one of the string beans, snapped off the ends, then broke it in two and dropped the halves into the colander. She reached for another bean, knowing Rose could see through her cellophane excuse.

Stopping Emily's nervous fussing with a gentle hand, Rose looked her straight in the eye. "You're right about Jess having no interest in the farm, god knows, he never knew much happiness here. But farm's farm and family's family. Jess loves you and Honey and he's always interested in what happens to the two of you. There's a huge difference there, my girl. Now, you go call your brother, and tell him your happy news."

Emily laid the bean back on the pile beside the colander, then glanced at first the phone, then Rose.

"Go on with you. Call him. Putting it off isn't going to make it any easier."

As usual, Rose was right. Emily went to the

phone and resolutely dialed Jesse's number. It rang once, twice, three times, then four. Emily was about to hang up in relief. The click of the receiver being lifted from its cradle on the other end stopped her.

"Hello."

The deep timbre of her brother's no-nonsense tone sent Emily's nerves off into a new tangle. It's a good thing she'd never planned on a career with the CIA. She just wasn't cut out for subterfuge.

"Hi, Jess."

"Emily? Is that you?"

"Yes, it's me."

"Is something wrong?"

"No, why would you think there was?"

"Your voice sounds strange."

She smiled, hoping it would seep into her voice and transmit through the wires to Jess. "Sorry. I guess my mind wandered for a second there."

"So, to what do I owe the honor of a phone call from my little sister?" When the silence stretched out and she didn't answer, Jesse became alarmed again. "There *is* something wrong. What is it?"

Taking a deep breath, Emily made up her mind to take the plunge. "It's nothing bad, Jess. It's just that I should have called you much sooner than this and now I'm afraid you're going to be upset with me, but honestly it wasn't because I didn't want you to—"

"Whoa! Slow down." His laughter did nothing to ease Emily's nerves. "When you babbled as a kid, it always meant you were hiding something you knew would get you into trouble." Silence. "So, want to tell me what mess you've managed to get yourself into this time?''

''I'm married.'' There. She'd said it.

''Married?'' His tone lightened and she could almost see his wide smile. ''I'd hardly call that a mess. That's wonderful, Em. I'm truly happy for you. Although, had I been placing bets on it, I'd have bet against you being the first of us to tie the knot.''

''You're forgetting Honey's marriage to Stan.''

Jess snorted in disgust. ''That jerk. I never counted that. She never would have married him, had it not been for—well, let's not get into that. So, who's the lucky guy?''

Her brother had never tried to hide his opinion of Stan, even after Honey married him. And Emily could still recall the shouting match Jess and her father had gotten into the night Honey announced she'd do what Frank Kingston decreed and marry the man he'd picked out for her.

''Em?''

''I married Kat Madison about a week ago.''

''Kat? I thought he'd disappeared years ago.''

''He came back.''

''And you two finally admitted what the rest of us have known for years. You love each other.'' The smile had returned to his voice. He sounded as if he was truly happy for her.

However, Emily was still concentrating on Jess's stunning revelation. Exactly how long had Kat occupied a special place in her heart, a place far different than the one she'd consigned him to for years? Had everyone guessed but her?

She glanced nervously at Rose. "Yes, something like that." She paused. "Jess, you aren't angry because I didn't tell you in time for you to be here, are you?"

"Me? Hell no. I've been on fire-tower duty for three months and wouldn't have been able to come anyway. In fact, you caught me just in time. I came home for a change of clothes and some other stuff and was just on my way back to the flora and fauna of the Adirondacks."

Emily passed a reassuring nod to Rose, who'd been watching her anxiously through the entire conversation. Rose gave her a thumbs-up and went back to her string beans.

A long, empty silence fell between brother and sister. She lowered her voice to keep Rose from hearing. "Jess? Are you sure?"

"I said so, didn't I? I couldn't be happier for both of you." Silence again.

She'd hurt him, made him feel like the outsider he'd always seen himself as. But knowing Jess, he'd never tell her. Sharing his pain was just not something he did.

"So, what's Kat doing these days?"

"He's fixing up his parents' house to sell it."

"I always loved the Madison house. It always seemed warmer than ours." Silence. Emily had no desire to bring up past hurts. "But that could have been because of the people in it, and you know that doesn't include you, Honey and Rose."

Again she let Jesse's statement pass without comment. Instead, she tried to veer the conversation away from the past. "Kat says he'll be done soon."

"Have him give me a call when he's settled on a price. I might have a buyer for him."

Emily's heart sank. If Jess had a buyer and the house sold as soon as Kat finished it, that would cut his only tie with his hometown.

"Em?"

"Yes, I'll tell him. Well, I better let you get back to work—"

"Em?"

"Yes?"

"Be happy, kid, and hang onto Kat. From what I recall from past encounters, and if he hasn't changed, he's good people. And damned handsome, too. You two will make show-stopping babies. Bye."

Before she could say anything more, he hung up.

"Bye." She replaced the receiver in its cradle, then leaned against the wall.

"Something wrong?"

Emily glanced at Rose's anxious expression. She forced a smile. "No. Everything's fine. Just fine." If you could define *fine* as finding out your whole family knew you were in love years before you did—or that you'd just hurt someone you loved.

As for keeping Kat, Jess had no way of knowing she wanted to hang onto Kat more than anything, but how do you hold onto a rolling stone? Especially when you've made it very clear that you don't want his prolonged presence in your life.

EVER SINCE that morning, with the exception of lunch under Rose's watchful eye, Emily had studiously avoided Kat all day. When he'd gone to the barn to check the new foal, she'd made a quick exit with an excuse about riding an inspection of the fences with Bert. When she'd returned and he'd tried to head her off, she'd taken off in the opposite direction.

After last night, he'd been sure they'd taken some gigantic steps toward a relationship based on more than a business agreement. Now, once more he wasn't sure where he stood. But he intended to find out. He still had plenty of light to finish putting up the sub-siding, but he wanted some answers from Emily and he wanted them now.

Toolbox in hand, he trudged purposefully across the back lawn, vaguely aware of the array of flowers lining either side of the back porch and perfuming the air with their heady scents. Taking the three wooden stairs to the porch in one stride, Kat opened the screen door and stopped dead.

Atop a wobbly stool, screwdriver in hand, Rose was intent on repairing the cabinet-door hinge. Quietly, so as not to scare her, Kat moved to stand beside the stool. With one deft movement, he grabbed Rose around the waist and set her on the floor.

"Mercy! You scared the tar out of me." Rose clasped her hand to the flowered bodice of her cotton housedress. "Emily was right. You came by that name of yours quite honestly."

"I'm sorry I frightened you, but watching you teetering up there did a pretty good job on my nerves, too. Now, what exactly were you doing on that stool?'' He placed his hands on his hips and glared at the woman who barely topped off at his shirt pocket.

''Fixing that darn hinge. The screw fell out a few months back. I kept asking Bert to fix it, but he never got to it. I'm tired of fitting the door back in the opening before I close it, so I decided I'd do it myself.''

''Well, now that I'm here,'' he said, taking the screwdriver from her, ''you let me take care of the handyman projects and you stick to cooking.'' He flashed what he hoped was a gentle smile. ''Emily would have both our hides if you took a header off that stool.''

For a long moment, Rose stared up at him, her eyes questioning something. His motives? ''Why don't I fix the cabinet, and you make us some coffee?''

She fidgeted with her apron, straightening it and checking the ties. ''Do you have time for a cup with an old woman?'' Despite her attempt at a light tone, Kat detected a hesitancy.

Hoping to relax her, Kat wriggled his eyebrows. ''I never pass up a chance to have a cup of coffee and a chat with a beautiful woman.''

Rose threw him a startled look. ''I certainly hope that doesn't apply to anyone other than your wife.''

He liked that Rose protected Emily, and more and more he liked Rose. ''Are there other beautiful women besides Emily and of course, you?'' He winked at her, but instead of smiling, she turned away and began fumbling with putting a filter in the basket of the coffeemaker, then filling it with coffee. "Oh, and I only pass up coffee if Emily makes it."

As she filled the carafe with water, Rose nodded and mumbled to herself. "Poor girl just hasn't a clue as to why people build kitchens on their houses."

He chuckled and began to screw in the hinge. "She's always been a foreigner in the kitchen. My mother once tried—"

The sound of glass smashing against the sink drew him away from his job. He hurried to her side.

"Are you okay?" Herding Rose out of the way, he took a paper towel and cleaned up the shards of glass scattered in the sink.

"Yes, I'm fine, but look what I've done," Rose exclaimed. "How clumsy. I'm afraid coffee will have to wait until I get a new carafe."

Kat threw the glass in the trash can. "Do you have any instant?"

She nodded, visibly working to pull herself together. "I got a jar for Emily before I left for vacation." She grinned weakly at him. "We're not the only ones who can't abide her coffee. She can't drink it herself."

A few minutes later, the hinge was secure and Kat and Rose were sipping instant coffee together at the table. Kat noted a sheet of paper with a list of things to do around the house.

"What's this?"

Seeming to have recovered from her accident but still showing signs of nerves, Rose took it from him and laid it aside. "It's a list I made for Bert before

I left for Mexico. I guess he was too busy with the horses to get to it.''

"If you leave it with me, I'll try to get some of them done for you. There's not really much here." He picked up the paper and read down the list. "A leaky faucet in the bathroom, a loose board on the porch stairs, a sticky closet door in your room. I can probably have them done in a day or two."

"That would be wonderful. Thank you."

Rose's voice sounded like she was talking to the local repair man and not the husband of her surrogate daughter. When he looked up, he found Rose studying him. He had to ask the question. "Rose, is there something about me that you don't like?"

Her eyes widened. "Lord, no. Whatever gave you that idea?"

"You're very uneasy around me and you keep looking at me as if…as if you're waiting for something that'll give you an excuse to tell me to hit the road."

Rose fussed with her apron, smoothing out imaginary wrinkles from the pristine material. "I can't imagine how you got such an idea."

"That's a relief. I thought maybe you didn't think too much of Emily's choice in husbands."

She looked at him from beneath lowered lashes, then tucked a strand of gray hair into the bun at her nape and raised her head, her expression serious. "I couldn't be happier about Emily's choice of husbands."

Despite her denial, he sensed Rose wasn't totally at ease with this new state of affairs. Kat wanted to press the subject, but he let it slide. Maybe it was just him and his own insecurities. Maybe even just nerves.

Let's face it, his nerves hadn't been in tip-top condition today. What with him trying to second-guess Emily's motives every time they got near each other, and now her new crusade to avoid him, he'd had good reason to be a bit edgy.

"Can I ask you something?"

He glanced over his cup at Rose. "Ask away."

She held up her hand. "This is really none of my business, so, if you don't want to answer, it's okay." Hesitating for a moment, she pulled a loose thread from her apron pocket, rolled it into a ball between her thumb and forefinger, then set it on the edge of her saucer. "Is there a problem with you and Emily?"

"Problem?" Where to start. While he silently categorized the problems he and Emily had, Kat tried to keep his face expressionless.

"I only ask because she doesn't seem like the typical happy bride. She never called me and never called her brother until today. That's not natural. She should be shouting her happiness from the rooftops." She leveled a look at him. "That is, unless she has reason not to."

Standing, Kat walked to the stove, put another spoonful of coffee granules in his cup, then poured hot water over them. Turning, he leaned one hip against the sink. Then, trying to look as nonchalant as possible so as to not bring about any more questions in Rose's head, he stirred the cup's contents.

"When have you ever known Emily to do things the way other people do them?" He kept his attention on the swirling brown liquid. "I think Em's a bit embarrassed by the speed with which we got married."

Very close to the truth, if not the truth, he told himself, feeling like a chump for lying to Rose when she was so concerned for Emily's happiness.

"But—" The phone rang. Rose sighed and went to answer it. "Yes. He's here. Just a moment." She held the receiver out to Kat. "It's for you."

He took it. "Hello."

"Madison, Pritchard here. I just got word that the old guy in the nursing home passed away this morning."

"HAD I KNOWN neither of you planned on eating enough to keep a bird off death's doorstep, I could have saved myself a lot of work today." Rose glanced from Kat to Emily.

Emily looked at her plate. String beans and mashed potatoes that should have shared the plate with a slice of meat loaf, were stirred together into a very unappetizing mixture. From beneath her lashes, she checked out Kat's plate and found it a twin to her own.

What did he have to be upset about? She was the one who'd seduced him and ended up putting her heart on the line to be trampled. For him this was just a job, much like any other job he'd done before he hit the road to the next one. For her it was the rest of her life without him.

Kat pushed his plate back. "I'm sorry, Rose. My appetite seems to have taken a vacation."

"Well, wherever it is, it's in good company. Emily's seems to have vanished with it." She looked from one to the other. "Either of you want to talk about whatever it is that's ruined my perfectly good meal?"

Kat glanced at both of them, then stood and walked out of the house, leaving Emily and Rose to stare after him. Emily's gaze remained fixed on the doorway. She'd never seen Kat act this way. His departure was downright rude, and bad manners didn't fit into Kat's makeup. If anything, he always went out of his way to be accommodating and polite.

"What about you?"

Startled out of her thoughts, Emily turned to Rose. "I'm just not hungry. Guess I overate at lunch." She gestured toward the door through which Kat had disappeared. "Any idea what's wrong with him?"

Rose shook her head, but that she too was worried about him showed plainly on her features. "He got a phone call late this afternoon, and ever since then, he hasn't said more than a dozen words."

"Do you know who the call was from?"

"A private investigator."

What could Kat want with a private investigator? Was he in some kind of trouble? She'd never seen him so upset before. Maybe if she went to him, he'd talk about it. Maybe it was her turn to help him. She stood. Rose grabbed her arm.

"Do you think it's good a idea to press him?"

Emily smiled and patted her friend's hand. "Someone has to. He's obviously being eaten up inside. He needs to get it out." Pushing her chair back, she headed out the back door toward the sound of hammering.

EMILY APPROACHED the Madison house quietly. Perched atop an aluminum extension ladder with a battery-operated light to illuminate what he was doing, Kat held a board in place with one hand and pounded nails with an unaccustomed vengeance with the other. She scanned the progress he'd made. He was very close to being finished and that meant it wouldn't be long before he would put the house up for sale. Then...

The thought settled into the pit of her stomach like a lead weight. Once the house sold, how long would it be before he picked up and left again? She recalled the emptiness of finding her best friend had just disappeared from her life before. The feelings she experienced now were not unlike what she'd felt then. Desolation, pain and apprehension rocked her world.

She'd gone on without Kat then, but could she go one without him this time, especially if she might be carrying his child?

While her heart cried out its silent protest, her gaze rested on the man she loved. Because she'd be risking too much if she said it aloud, she told him silently of her feelings, of what he meant to her, of how much she needed him in her life, in their child's life. In doing so, she finally admitted that always and forever, the other half of Emily Kingston was Kat Madison.

Kat reached for another handful of nails. Since receiving the call from Pritchard's office, he'd felt as empty inside as he had the day he'd found the cradle and the adoption papers. Where did he go from here?

The old man was his last connection with his birth parents. Another nail entered the board with two fierce blows from the hammer. He'd gone down every road and explored every possibility. Two more nails were driven home. Maybe he was never meant to find them. The hammer found its mark on another nail. He paused and rested the hammer on his thigh. Lowering his head, he made an admission that had been haunting him for days.

Maybe he should have just stayed here sixteen years ago and forgotten about tracking down two people who obviously didn't want to be found.

Slowly, he crawled down the ladder. Having vented his frustration, he threw the hammer to the ground, then turned. Emily stood an arm's length beyond him, her face etched in concern, her body bathed in silver moonlight.

She came to him, wordlessly, and laid her fingers on his lips, silencing any words he might have said.

He looked down at her, searching her gaze. The moonlight glinted off something lying against her skin at the neck of her blouse. His heart did a double beat. It was the necklace he'd given her for her thirteenth birthday. She'd kept it. No matter how she'd felt about him, she'd kept it.

He lifted it with one fingertip. Then looked into her eyes. "Why?"

"Because a friend gave it to me as token of our relationship."

"But that friend walked out on you without a word."

"But he came back." At that moment she knew she'd forgiven him. Now if she could just learn to trust him. But that wasn't why she'd followed him. "Talk to me, Kat. What's wrong?"

He shook his head and tried to turn away, but she held fast.

"No. Not this time. I won't let you walk away again. This time we're going to talk." She smiled. "And you know me when I make up my mind to do something."

She could read the indecision in his expression.

"There's nothing you can do. Nothing anyone can do."

Her heart felt as if someone had reached into her chest and squeezed it. His pain became her pain. She would give her life to erase the hopelessness from his voice.

"Let me try." She barely felt the hot tears rolling down her cheeks. Tears for him and tears for her. "You owe me that much," she whispered. "Please, let me try."

For a long time, he stared down at her, then he nodded and swept her into his arms. "It's time you knew."

Relief flooded through her. Standing on tiptoe, she pressed her lips to his. "Let's go home."

Chapter Eleven

Kat had thought that it would be easier to tell Emily his secret here, in the privacy of her room, in the dark, with her nestled close to his side in the big bed. He'd been wrong. All the demons that had haunted him since the day he'd found the damning evidence of his biological parents' abandonment lurked in the shadows. All the doubts and insecurities of having been pushed from their lives, the ones he'd been sure he'd overcome, were still with him.

Emily stirred beside him. She slid her leg over his and tightened her arm around his waist.

"Em, are you asleep?"

"No."

"You're very quiet."

"I'm waiting."

No need to ask what for. She wanted the explanation for him running out on her and for his unforgivable behavior earlier in the kitchen. And as much as he hated to face what she might think of him afterward, he finally admitted she deserved to know. He should have told her that first day. If he hadn't been such a coward, he would have.

But to have to face Emily's condemnation was something he didn't want to even think about. It would have been bad enough then, before he knew how he felt about her. But now…

"Do you remember the day of my parent's funeral?"

"Yes. It was the day you disappeared."

The sadness in her voice, a sorrow he'd caused, tore through him. He squeezed her closer. "I left the cemetery and went back to the house. I don't know why. I guess maybe I just wanted to be close to something familiar, something they loved."

Emily made no comment. She lay very still, as if hanging on his next word.

"The only part of the house that had been destroyed was the living room and the spare room above it. Their room was intact, so I went there." He drew a deep breath. "When I started looking around, I found some things in the closet that…"

"Yes? What did you find?"

"A wooden cradle and a small metal box."

She propped herself on one elbow. He could barely see her in the darkness. "Is that the cradle in your room?"

"Yes."

"What was in the box?"

"Papers. Their marriage license. My diploma. My baptismal papers. And my…." The words stuck in his throat. "…my adoption papers and a note from a Methodist minister telling how I'd been left on his doorstep, abandoned by my parents.''

''Abandoned? Adoption papers? I don't understand.''

The disdain he'd expected to hear in Emily's voice wasn't there. Only shock and confusion.

''I'm not the biological son of Hilda and Charles Madison. They adopted me when I was an infant.''

She frowned. ''I don't see what this has to do with you leaving all those years ago or why you walked out tonight without a word.''

He let go of her and sat up. Looping his arms around his raised knees, he gazed into the darkness. ''I couldn't face anyone.''

She knelt next to him, close enough for her warm breath to brush his bare shoulder. ''Why? What difference did it make? You were still you.''

''That's just it. I wasn't me.''

''So you ran.'' No accusation colored her words, just resigned understanding.

''No, not really. I just left. The only thing I could think of was finding my real parents. Finding them and asking them why they'd deserted me.'' He turned to her. ''Don't you see? I didn't know who I was anymore. Rian Madison was a lie.''

''Rian Madison was my best friend.'' She laid her hand on his arm. ''Best friends believe in each other.''

Emotions rose up in him so strongly he felt that they'd choke him. He should have known Emily would react this way. She'd never judged people by who they were, just what they were. Why hadn't he seen that back then?

Still, even knowing that and seeing the understanding on her face, he couldn't completely let go, tell her the deep-down hurt the discovery had caused, the anxiety of years of searching, the ache of unanswered questions. Maybe someday he would, but not now when talking about it had opened the wound and left him raw again.

He was barely aware of Emily leaving the bed until the room flooded with light. Emily had turned on the light, and, as with every other time that Emily had been in his life, the demons had disappeared.

Before him stood his wife, the most beautiful sight in the world to him, even in that makeshift, *sexy* nightgown with the raveled hem and the cutout sleeves. She was his Em, his peace of mind, his haven from pain, his friend. Why hadn't he seen that all those years ago? If he'd come to her then instead of running away, would things have been different? Would she have learned to love him? She moved to him, and he caressed her cheek with the back of his hand.

The private investigator made sense to Emily now, but she wanted to hear it from Kat. "What about that phone call today? Rose said it was after you got it that you changed."

He sighed and lay back against the pillows. She came to join him, kneeling at his side on the patchwork coverlet. "I had a P.I. looking into finding my parents. They'd found an old man who might have known something. The call today was to tell me that he'd died.'' He glanced at her. ''He was my last hope. There's nowhere else to go now.''

Emily could feel the pain radiating from Kat. His voice held such wrenching despair. What could she say? No words could erase the facts. All she knew how to do was offer herself and her love.

She lay down beside him and enveloped him in her embrace. He turned to her and held her close, as if drawing strength from her, and she allowed him to take all he needed.

From his first touch, Emily knew that this wasn't going to be like the last time they'd made love. He touched her with a new gentleness, a tenderness born of need. He cradled her body like a fragile vase, as if fearing that the slightest bit of roughness would break her and he'd be left alone.

Desire and passion raged from both of them, but with a new sweetness, a new meaning. He held her as if he never wanted to be separated from her again. And, oh, how she wanted to believe that. Needed to believe it.

For herself, she tried to give him the one thing he seemed to need above all else right now, the feeling of belonging, of mattering to someone. It wasn't hard. She just let her love guide her.

When it was over, Kat slept, but Emily lay wide awake staring up at the dark ceiling. Now, she knew for certain she'd lose Kat again. He'd fulfill his promise to her, then he'd leave. How, when this place held so much pain and bitterness for him, could he stay here? The kindest thing she could do would be to help him get away from here as soon as possible and break her own heart in the process.

THE BATHROOM DOOR closed behind Emily, shutting out the world and closing her into a world of pink wallpaper and white porcelain. She looked down at the box she'd gotten at the drugstore. If she was pregnant, she'd know in a very short time. Then she'd tell Kat he had kept his end of the bargain and was free to go.

If not… Well, she'd face that problem when she had to.

She removed the small, rectangular, white plastic box from the package. Following the directions exactly, she proceeded to do the pregnancy test.

After the longest ten minutes of her life, she checked the results. A pink minus. She wasn't pregnant. Her heart plummeted.

A mixture of confusing emotions exploded inside her. Disappointment that she wasn't pregnant followed quickly on the heels of an odd sense of relief that she wouldn't have to face the responsibilities of motherhood just yet. Elation that Kat wouldn't leave yet warred with regret that she couldn't give him the news that would free him to move on, away from the house that had caused him such pain.

She sank down on the side of the tub and buried her head in her hands. Tears flowed down her cheeks. Why in blazes was she crying? Hells bells, didn't this mean that Kat would be staying for a while longer, that she'd be able to accumulate more memories for the time when he did leave? More memories to tear her heart to pieces, just like before, only this time, it would be much worse because she loved him.

For a woman who knew what she wanted and who seldom, if ever, cried, she sure was falling to pieces fast. Sitting up straight, she grabbed a tissue and swiped away all traces of the tears.

After carefully stowing the remnants of the test in the trash, she left the bathroom and started down the hall. She might as well break the news to him. Seeing Kat's door open, she slowed her pace and peeked in.

At the side of the bed, Kat sat on the floor polishing the cradle. His movements were so gentle, so concentrated, it was as if by sheer touch he could make the connection he'd lost as a baby. She cleared her throat.

"So that's it, huh?" What else could she say?

"Yup. Whoever made it did a great job." He turned it so she could see the end. "Look at this workmanship."

From behind Emily came a gasp and the crash of glass hitting the floor and shattering into a million pieces. She jumped and spun around.

Rose stood there, eyes wide and riveted on Kat. Around her feet lay the remains of a crystal vase and the broken stems of a bouquet of mixed flowers.

"Rose! What is it?" Emily rushed to Rose's side.

Even as she watched, Rose's face lost all color and her knees began to buckle. Emily reached for her. An instant later Kat scooped Rose into his arms and carried her into her room. He laid her on the bed. Emily and he stood over her.

"Get a cold cloth," he instructed.

Her heart beating wildly and her brain trying to register what had just happened, Emily ran to do his bidding. By the time she came back with the wet washcloth, Rose was stirring. Gently, Emily draped the cloth over the woman's forehead.

"That's it. You, my good woman, are going to the doctor. This is the second time you've had a spell like this since you got back from Mexico. No telling what you got down there." Emily fought to keep her voice steady.

Kat took her hand while they waited for Rose to speak.

"A doctor won't be necessary. I'm just a bit faint. I'm feeling better all ready." She struggled to sit up, but Kat laid his hand on her shoulder.

"Just lie still for a while. We don't need you taking another nosedive to the floor." He smiled gently.

Rose looked up at him. Her eyes held an expression that Emily had never seen before. She couldn't identify it, but Rose hadn't taken her gaze off Kat since he spoke.

"Can I get you anything? Water?" Emily suddenly felt more than helpless, she felt downright intrusive.

Blinking, Rose tore her gaze from Kat. "No, dear. I'm fine. Really. Now, you two stop all this fussing." She sat up.

Hearing the voice of the woman who had always been her leaning post quaver, Emily doubted the validity of her statement. But knowing Rose's stubborn streak, she stepped away to make room for the older woman to swing her legs over the edge of the white lace coverlet.

"If you'll just go about your business, I'll sit here for a minute and make sure my head is back in order." Rose glanced from Kat to Emily.

Not sure what to do, she sent Kat a questioning glance. He nodded. "Okay, we'll go, but you make sure you don't move until you feel up to it."

Smiling at Kat, Rose nodded. "I will." They'd nearly made it to the door when Rose spoke again.

"Kat, where did you get the...cradle?"

Kat's expression froze. Emily could see his jaw working. He didn't want to explain, but she had no idea how he'd sidestep Rose's question.

"I've had it since I was a baby." He glanced at Emily, then back to Rose. "I was found in it after my parents abandoned me on a church doorstep." His last words could have rivaled steel for their rigidity.

"So you don't know who your parents are?" Rose's voice was quiet, her question almost a whisper.

"No. And I don't care to know them any more than they cared to know me." Kat turned and stalked from the room.

Staring after him, Emily could imagine how much that cost him to admit. When she turned back to Rose, the woman's face had paled again. She rushed to her.

"It's all right, dear. Perhaps you and Kat were

right. I think I'll just lie here for a while and get my bearings.'' She lay back on the pillows and rolled over so that Emily was left staring at her back.

BY THE FOLLOWING MORNING, Kat's good humor had been restored. Emily, however, suspected that the identity of his biological parents ate at Kat a lot more than he'd admit.

Showered and dressed, she hurried downstairs to help Rose with the breakfast dishes before she went out to the barns. Even though Rose had protested that she was feeling fine, Emily still worried that Rose should see the doctor. Perhaps she'd picked up something on her vacation and it had taken this long to manifest itself. It did seem as if each spell she had was getting more severe than the last.

As she walked into the kitchen, she found Rose drying the last of the dishes.

"I told you to wait for me and I'd help you with them."

"Oh, goodness. There were only a few and it was easier for me to just do them than to wait for you." Opening the cabinet, Rose put away a stack of plates. "Besides, you have your own chores. I've been doing this for a good many years without your help. Why do you suddenly feel that I need it now?"

"Yesterday—"

"Yesterday I was a silly woman with a bit of light-headedness, nothing more." She held her arms wide. "Look at me. Fit as a fiddle."

"I want you to do what Kat asked and see a doctor.'' Having grown up with Rose's mulish nature, Emily set herself for a battle of wills.

''Oh, and I have no say in this.''

''No, you don't.'' She stood nose-to-nose with her surrogate mother.

Placing her hands on her hips, Rose dug in. ''I'm still older than you, young lady, and you'll not tell me what to do.''

''Is this a private battle or can anyone join in?''

Emily and Rose swung toward the voice. Honey stood in the kitchen doorway, her shoulder leaning against the doorjamb, enjoying the spectacle. ''I'm just glad I sent my son over to talk to Kat. I'd hate for him to see two grown women acting like children.''

''Will you tell this pigheaded woman that passing out at the drop of a hat is not normal and that she needs to see a doctor? Maybe coming from a nurse, she'll believe it.'' Emily pulled a chair from beneath the table and plopped down into it. ''I can't seem to get through to her.''

Honey's playful expression turned to instant concern. ''Is that right, Rose? Having you been passing out?''

Rose folded her wet dish towel and hung it over the handle of the oven to dry. ''Of course not. Your sister can make a scratch sound like a life-threatening wound, always could. I had a couple of bouts of light-headedness, that's all.''

''Oh, yes, just a couple,'' Emily chimed in. ''The last being severe enough that Kat had to carry her to her room, where, I might add, she spent the remainder of the afternoon yesterday.''

Honey took Rose firmly by the arm and led her to a seat at the table. ''I agree with Emily. You should see a doctor.''

Glaring at her, Rose shook her head. ''I do not need to see a doctor.''

''If you're scared of what he'll find,'' Honey offered, ''don't be. It could something as simple as you being anemic. No biggie. All you'll do is take a daily iron supplement.''

Standing, Rose looked from one sister to the other. ''I know you both mean well and have my best interests at heart. But trust me, I do not need a doctor. There's no cure for what ails me and it's not medical.'' She strode from the room.

''Em, you need to talk to her. You can make her see reason.''

''Honey,'' Emily's gaze was fixed on the chair where Rose had been sitting, ''I believe her.''

''What? Why?''

''I don't know. I just do.'' She couldn't explain it, but for some reason, Emily knew that Rose's claim of not needing a doctor was valid. ''Call it a gut feeling. Of course, this in no way solves the problem. Something is bothering Rose and if it isn't physical, I'm going to find out exactly what it is.''

Shrugging her dismissal of the entire subject, Honey wandered to the refrigerator, then opened the door and extracted a can of orange soda. Popping the tab, she took a sip and studied Emily over the top of the can. Lowering the can, she set it on the counter, then wiped the moisture from her hands on a paper towel.

"So, how's the baby-making business going?"

Her sister's words jolted Emily out of her thoughts of Rose. "Uh, going?"

Honey came closer to Emily and bent to look her in the eye. "My god, you did it. I can tell by the look in your eye. You actually did it."

"Honey! Please. Keep your voice down. The entire world doesn't need to know that I went to bed with Kat." The heat of embarrassment crept up Emily's throat and fanned out across her cheeks. "And I'll thank you not to refer to it as a baby-making business."

"Are you going into the b-b-baby business with m-m-my uncle Kat?"

Danny's startled voice brought the two women around sharply.

"Ah, Danny, what are you doing here?" Terrific, thanks to Honey, now Emily's four-year-old nephew expected a rundown on her sex life.

"Mom s-s-said we couldn't s-s-stay long, s-s-so I came to s-s-see if she was ready to g-g-go. Aunt Emily, are you g-g-gonna make babies with Uncle Kat?"

Glaring at her sister, Emily turned to Danny and smiled sweetly. "Your mom will explain it on your way home, love." Striding purposefully to the back door, she swung it wide, then turned to her smirking sister. "Goodbye, Honey."

HONEY HAD NO SOONER LEFT than Emily made her way upstairs to Rose's room. This time she wasn't taking no for an answer. She wanted to know what was bothering Rose so much that it caused her to pass out, and she wasn't leaving until she found out. After all, the woman was like a mother to her, and if she couldn't share this with Emily who could she talk to?

Knocking softly on the door, she waited until she heard Rose call, "Come in."

When she stepped into the room, she found Rose lying on the bed. "Rose—"

"Now, don't go jumping to conclusions just because I'm lying down. I was thinking, and I needed to be comfortable." She threw Emily one of her obstinate looks.

Taking a seat beside her housekeeper, Emily took her hand. The familiar scent of Rose's lily of the valley perfume drifted up to her. As a child, she'd always found that fragrance comforting, synonymous with security and love. "I wasn't going to jump to conclusions. I just came up to tell you I believe you."

Rose's eyes opened wide. "You do?"

"Yes. But now I want to know what's really bothering you." When Rose would have spoken, Emily held up her hand to stop her. "Don't even think about saying nothing. I'm not leaving until you spill the beans. So start talking."

For a long time, Rose stared at Emily, as if waiting for her to back down. "I'm sorry, dear, but this is personal."

"Personal?" Emily couldn't believe her ears.

"We've never had secrets from each other. We've always talked about everything."

"Have we?" Rose looked at Emily.

Emily squirmed. Had Rose guessed the real reason she and Kat had married? *Hell and damnation!* She never was good at this kind of thing. She ran the conversations she'd had with Rose through her head, searching for anything that might have tipped her off to the real reason she'd become Emily Madison. Nothing came to mind. But she must have done something to give it away.

Kat! He'd been with her earlier. Maybe he'd said something. "Did Kat say something to upset you?"

"No. He's a fine young man." Rose's smile looked very much like that of the cat that ate the cream.

"Then what is it that has you so upset you keep passing out on me?" She had no desire to agitate Rose any more than she obviously was, but she felt so helpless.

Rose stared at her for a long time, as if trying to make up her mind about something. She rolled to her side, turning her back to Emily, then rolled back. In her hands she clutched a box made of dark wood.

Emily glanced at the box and then at Rose. Large tears rolled down her cheeks. Emily took her dear friend in her arms.

"Rose, I can't stand seeing you this unhappy. Please tell me what's wrong."

Sniffing, then pulling from Emily's grasp, Rose extracted an embroidered handkerchief from her apron pocket, then wiped her nose. "It's a long story, child and I'm afraid not a very pretty one."

"Tell me. Please. Maybe if you get it out, you'll feel better."

"Nothing will ever make what I've done better, child, nothing."

"What has that box got to do with this?" Emily couldn't imagine this gentle, loving woman having done anything as bad she seemed to think she had.

"It's my jewelry box. My father had it made for me when I turned sixteen. I've kept it all these years."

Smiling gently, Emily's gaze flickered to the box, then back to Rose. "That's sweet."

"I want you to have it."

"But it's yours. You've kept it all this time." She took the jewelry box from Rose and set it on the night table. "You just keep it in here and that way you'll still have it, and I can admire it when I come to your room."

Before she could say anything, Rose glanced at the box. Fresh tears formed in her clear blue eyes. "You don't understand. I want you to have it because I'll be leaving at the end of the month."

Chapter Twelve

"Leaving?" Emily couldn't believe her ears. "But why?"

Glancing out her bedroom window toward the Madison house, Rose smiled. "You don't need me anymore."

She followed Rose's gaze to the window. "Don't need you? That's crazy. Of course I need you." Emily didn't even try to hide the desperation in her voice at the thought of Rose not being a part of her life.

"No you don't." Rose laid a hand on Emily's shoulder and squeezed. "You have a husband who loves you and who will take very good care of you."

Whether or not Kat loved her was not something Emily wanted to think about right now. Too scary, too impossible, too...wonderful to even contemplate. Keeping the closest thing to a mother that she'd ever known, that's what she had to think about now. "It's the doctor thing, right?" She grabbed Rose's hand. "I told you I believe that there's nothing physically wrong with you. You don't have to go to the doctor if you don't want to.''

Patting the hand holding hers, Rose kissed Emily's cheek. ''No, it's not the doctor thing. Besides, I never put much stock in doctors, anyway.''

Emily paced beside the white-lace-covered double bed. As she walked, she battled with tears that wanted to fall partly from frustration, but mostly because, unless she came up with some answers really fast, she was about to lose a beloved friend. ''None of this makes any sense.''

''Emily, I—''

Emily grabbed both of Rose's hands in hers. ''Please tell me. I can make it all right, if you just tell me what's wrong.''

A weak smile curved Rose's pale lips. ''I wish it was that easy. I—'' The faint sound of pounding coming from the Madison house stopped her words. ''He's such a fine man, Emily. It does my heart good to see that.''

''Rose, please. Forget Kat. I want to know what has happened in the last few days that makes you want to leave.'' As hard and as much as she searched her memory, Emily could not come up with a reason for Rose's decision. Since it had come out of the blue, it had to be something that had happened recently.

Rose's smile actually turned bright. ''Ah, but we *are* talking about Kat.''

Frowning, Emily glanced toward the window, then back to Rose. ''I'm really lost now. You said he didn't say anything to upset you.''

"He didn't."

"Then what does he have to do with any of this?"

Going to the night table, Rose picked up the wooden jewelry box. Clasping it to her chest with one hand, while running the other over the shiny wood surface, she sniffed loudly. "I can't stand to see your heart breaking like this." She looked away from the jewelry box and into Emily's tearful gaze. "You have to promise me that you won't mention what I'm going to tell you to anyone, most of all Kat."

"But—"

Rose looked into her eyes imploringly. "Promise. If you don't I won't tell you anything."

Baffled, Emily nodded. "I promise. But why all the mystery?"

"I've carried this burden alone for a good many years and maybe it's time I shared the load." She collapsed wearily on the bed and motioned for Emily to join her. When she had, Rose laid the jewelry box in Emily's lap.

Blinded by the surge of her emotions, Emily stared unseeingly at the box, acutely aware of Rose's wavering voice.

"My father called me his little rosebud." With her forefinger, Rose lovingly traced the design on the lid. Tears rolled down her cheeks, hitting the box and creating large, dark spots on the wood. "When I got pregnant, he had the cradle made with the same design."

Comprehension seared its way through Emily's gut like a white-hot poker. She looked between Rose and the box several times before shaking her head. This couldn't be. Of all the things Emily could have guessed might be bothering Rose, this was definitely not one of them. Even to think it was insane, but she couldn't stop herself from saying the words.

"You're Kat's mother."

It wasn't a question. Just a statement of fact.

Rose's shoulders slumped. "I thought the day he first introduced himself that it was possible, but I didn't know for sure until I saw the cradle." She looked at Emily. "There's only one like that in the world and that's the one my son was in when I—" The tears began anew, this time wrenched from Rose in deep, horrible, agonizing sobs.

Feeling utterly helpless, Emily set the box aside. She longed to ask her why, why had she abandoned her child? Instead, she gathered Rose in her arms and did the only thing she could, let her cry it out.

"Now...you must...see...why...why I have to...go."

Emily understood. Rose couldn't live here with Kat, knowing he was her son and knowing he hated her for what she'd done. But what about Kat?

While Rose sobbed into her shoulder, Emily thought about Kat and what he'd do and say when he found out. How would he take it? But she'd promised Rose she wouldn't tell him.

Then she recalled how well he and Rose had gotten along right from the start. They had a genuine fondness for each other, that, given time and opportunity, could turn to love. Slowly, Rose's sobs subsided.

Emily took the distraught woman's shoulders and set her away from her. "You can't run away from this. You have to tell him. He deserves to know who you are."

Wide-eyed, Rose pulled out of Emily's grasp and shook her head vehemently. "No! Absolutely not. I can't stay. He hates me. He has a new life with you. I can't hurt him any more than I have already."

"Rose—"

"No! And you must promise me that you won't tell him either." Grabbing Emily's hand in a surprisingly iron grip, Rose stared imploringly into Emily's eyes. "Please. Promise me."

Reluctantly, Emily renewed her vow of silence, but wondered how she could keep something like this from Kat. "But I don't understand how this could happen. Whatever could have made you abandon your child?"

Knowing Rose and her huge capacity for love as she did, Emily knew it had to have been something drastic. Rose loved all kids. Emily couldn't conceive of anything that would make her willingly part with her own flesh and blood. As for herself, she knew in her heart that, if it were her child, she would go to any lengths for it, no matter how much pain and heartache it caused her. Perhaps this was the case with Rose.

Releasing her grip on Emily's hand, Rose dipped her head, as if unable to look at Emily while she related the story. "When I was eighteen, I met a man passing through our little town. His name was Andrew Bennett. I was young and impressionable and he was darkly handsome, worldly and exciting. It took an afternoon in his company for me to fall head over heels in love with him. And, to my total amazement, he said he loved me, too." She smiled wistfully. "I was so flattered."

She sniffed, then extracted a tissue from a box on her night table. Blowing her nose, she dropped it in the wastebasket. "My parents didn't like him. He was older than me by ten years." She paused as if expecting Emily to comment. When she didn't, feeling conversation might keep Rose from telling her the whole story, Rose went on.

"Anyway, one thing led to another and I found myself pregnant. He seemed as happy about the child as I was and promised to marry me. My parents flew into a rage and told me that all he wanted from me was sex. I argued that he loved me and I wanted to marry him. They said, since I was of age, if I wanted him, then they couldn't stop me, but they wouldn't consider me their daughter any longer."

Rose pulled another tissue from the box. This time, she crumpled it in her hands, as if even its flimsy substance would give her something solid to hang onto. "I believed them, but I loved Andy more than I respected their wishes." She glanced at Emily. "Can you understand that, child?"

She understood all right. If someone put a choice between them and Kat to her, she had no doubt which way she'd go. "Yes." Emily covered Rose's hands, silently encouraging her to go on.

"So, I ran off with him." She laughed lightly and without humor. "My parents were wrong. Andy and

I were married.'' Her shaking fingers shredded the tissue. ''I wrote to tell them they had a grandson. They never wrote back. Then one day the cradle came. No note, just the cradle. I'd hoped that meant they'd forgiven me, but I never knew. Andy had begun gambling and hanging around with a very shady crowd. By the time I summoned enough courage to say something, his gambling losses had us deeply in debt.''

She stood and began wringing her hands and pacing the mauve carpeting. ''To save himself from their threats, when one of his crowd was caught by the FBI, Andrew turned state's evidence. We began receiving threats, threats to Andrew, to me and to our son, so the FBI put us in the Witness Protection Program.''

Rose stopped beside Emily. Her eyes pleaded for understanding. Emily forced her lips into a smile. She gave an encouraging nod.

''I couldn't put Joey in jeopardy, nor could I ask him to grow up in an atmosphere like that, full of secrecy, lies and stealth, never knowing from one day to the next if we'd be discovered and have to pull up stakes and move on. So, the night before we entered the Program, I put him in his cradle and took him to a Methodist church parsonage upstate, rang the doorbell and hid. I waited outside to make sure someone found him, then I went with Andy to our new life—if that's what it could be called.'' She bowed her head. ''I just left my ten-month-old son on a stranger's doorstep and walked away.''

Her tears began anew. Emily remained silent, allowing her to cry it out.

Though Rose seemed to be waiting for it, there was no need for Emily to condemn her. The tone of the poor woman's voice and the heart-wrenching sound of her friend's sobs told Emily that Rose had tried, convicted and sentenced herself long ago.

She began pacing again. "We were in hiding for months before the trial was set. Then, just before the trial date, the gambler tried to escape and was killed. The FBI released us from the Program. We wanted to find our son, but before we could start looking, Andrew died in a car accident." She took a deep breath. "I began looking for Joey alone. But when I went back to the church, there were no records of my baby. I went from government office to government office for eighteen years, trying to get sealed records opened."

Rose walked to the window and pulled back the lace curtain. "I finally traced him here, to Bristol, New York." Her voice faded and she let the curtain drop back into place. "By the time I got here, Joey had left home and his adoptive parents were dead. I asked around, but no one knew where he'd gone."

"Is that when you came here?" Emily recalled how distraught Rose had been on that first day. Now, she knew why.

"Yes. I saw the ad for a housekeeper and cook at Clover Hills Farm in the local paper. Hoping that maybe he'd come back here one day, I took the job. What better place to wait than right next door? The rest you know.'' She glanced at Emily. ''Now, do you understand why I have to leave?''

Emily went to her. ''No, I don't. You did nothing wrong, and when Kat hears your story, he'll understand. You said yourself, he's a good man.''

''Even a good man has his limits, child. I'll be leaving at the end of the month.''

That left Emily just a few weeks to find a way to change Rose's mind.

EMILY LEANED BACK against the gnarled trunk of the ancient oak tree. It had been years since she'd come here. Fingering the tiny key on her necklace, she stared at the ground.

If she turned slightly to her right, she knew she'd find two entwined hearts carved into the tree. She and Kat had put them there when she was barely ten. In each heart was a set of initials, an & sign and below that a question mark. Little had she known back then who that question mark represented.

Little had she known back then that one day she'd come here to sit and try to untangle her life. All she wanted to do was help Rose, have her baby and live her life. The last thing she'd needed or wanted was to be the keeper of a secret that could influence the lives of the two people she loved most in the world.

Why had she promised not to tell Kat? Easily answered. If she hadn't, Rose would not have related her story. And now that she knew that story, what did she do about it? Could she break her promise?

All her life Emily had been thrown broken promises until she'd come to regard anyone else's promise as about as substantial as a wisp of smoke. However, she'd always kept hers. To her, a promise was akin to an oath in blood. But what if that promise hurt people? What if keeping it meant perpetuating that hurt?

If telling meant possible happiness for someone, was that considered breaking a promise?

She knew she owed allegiance to Rose, but what about Kat? She loved him. Did love supercede a promise? Didn't he deserve to put closure to a part of his life that haunted him daily?

Her father's words played through her head. *Some promises are made to be broken, little girl.* Was this one of them?

Emily plucked a buttercup from the grass beside her and began ruthlessly tearing off the sunny yellow petals, one by one. The sweet smell of the flower drifted up to her.

When she and Kat were kids, they'd hold buttercups under each other's chins to see if their wishes would come true. If it reflected yellow, which it always did, then the wish would come true.

A deep sigh issued from her. If only everyone could stay as young and innocent and free from worries as they'd been back then. But they couldn't. And flowers couldn't grant wishes. If they could, she'd have a solution to her problem. She threw the flower down.

"That's hardly the way to treat a flower that can make your every dream come true."

Kat's deep voice above her startled her. Damn his

cat-like step. "That's just a child's musing. I quit believing in that stuff long ago." She frowned up at him. "How did you know where to find me?"

He folded his long legs under him and sat beside her, his back against the tree. "Easy. I thought about where you always went to hide when we were kids." He paused, as if expecting her to comment. "So, what are you hiding from today?"

"I'm not hiding. I just need some time to myself." How could she tell him what was really bothering her and still keep her word to Rose? "I talked to Jesse," she said, hoping to guide him onto safe ground. "He said when you're ready to sell the house to call him. He might have a buyer for you."

Kat continued to study her. "Thanks. I will."

She squirmed under his scrutiny. His shoulder brushed hers. Her skin tingled. She scooted aside, leaving a space between them.

"Okay, Em. You've been avoiding me all day. Let's talk."

Taken by surprise, she grabbed at the first defense that entered her mind. "After you walked out on us at dinner, then made your speech in Rose's room, I didn't think you wanted company."

"Sorry. I'm not buying. You started avoiding me long before either of those events. Now, tell me what's up."

He pulled a handful of grass and selected one long thick blade. Cupping it between the sides of his thumbs, he blew into it. A high-pitched wail emerged, much like something a wounded animal would make.

She had no intention of getting into an argument with him. "I haven't been avoiding you. I've had work to do and so have you. It just happened to be in two different places."

No way would she admit that their intense love-making had so rattled her that she promised herself it had been the last. She was getting in too deep and she had to save herself before he left and the flood of loneliness swamped her.

Kat sat up and glared at her. She'd felt emotionally safer when she couldn't see his face. "Emily, your mixed signals are making me crazy."

"Signals?" This time, she had to admit, she had no idea what he was talking about.

"Yes, signals. One minute you're seducing me, the next you're ignoring me."

Standing, she moved away from him. Even angry, the temptation to fall into his arms and beg him to make love to her again was too great. And the last person she could count on to keep things under control was herself.

"You were imagining things. I seduced you, as you so crudely put it, because we have a business arrangement, and you'd left the time and place to initiate it to me. Please, don't make more of it than it is."

She never heard him coming and only realized he was next to her when he spun her by the shoulders to face him. "Bull. You can't tell me that the woman I made love to had nothing more than business on her mind."

Moving her gaze to his shirt front, Emily stiffened

against his touch. ''That's exactly what I'm telling you.''

''Then tell me while you're looking me in the eye.''

''Kat, I—''

''In the eye, Emily.''

Slowly, she raised her gaze to meet his. She could see herself reflected in his dark eyes. For a moment she felt as if he'd taken her inside him, made her his in some way, trapping her forever. She wanted to believe that. But her logical side told her she was dreaming.

Hardening her resolve and drawing on every bit of strength she had, she spoke the words that she hoped would convince him. ''It was only business.''

Kat let his hands fall from her shoulders and backed away. A vivid memory, too strong to dismiss, of a night of passion with a woman who responded with more fire than Kat had ever experienced before, belied her words.

''I don't believe you.''

He couldn't. If he hadn't been there, hadn't felt her fire, seen her passion explode inside her, heard her soft moans of satisfaction, then maybe he'd believe her. But not when his gut told him something totally different.

''That's too bad.'' She looked away. ''Of course, I can't prove it. You'll just have to take my word for it or not.''

''Not.''

For heaven's sake, she couldn't even look at him and say these things. And she expected him to believe her? Either he was totally wrong, or Emily was selling herself a bill of goods. Only one way to find out.

Two quick steps and he pulled her to him and covered her mouth with his. Her body stiffened, but her lips lay rigid and unresponsive beneath his. This would have warded him off, except for one thing she couldn't hide, the frantic beating of her heart against his chest. He tightened his embrace and deepened the kiss.

As if she knew what he was up to, she started struggling, pushing her fists against his chest. All the time her mouth grew softer and softer, belying her struggle for freedom. He loosened his hold, but she had already sagged against him. She fisted her hands in his shirt.

Freeing her mouth, she buried her face in his shirt front. "Damn you. Damn you," she mumbled into the fabric. Her hands dove beneath his shirt. Palms flattened, she explored his chest, rib cage and back. All the time she kept repeating her mantra. "Damn you."

High above them a small bird took to the air, frightened by their feverish movements. "I've been damned before. Once more won't make any difference."

Gently, he picked her up, then laid her in the grass. She clutched at him, not wanting him to leave her. He smiled. "Don't fret, Squirt. I'm not going anywhere. But I have to know that this is what you want. If it isn't, I won't lay a finger on you until you say so."

She smiled up at him, a seductive twist to her lips. Licking her lower lip, she arched her back, silently offering herself. He accepted.

The tiny white buttons on her cotton shirt slid easily from their anchors. One by one, he freed them. Inch by inch, her tanned flesh came into view. Fumbling with the front clasp on her bra like an adolescent on his first date, he finally snapped that free as well.

Sliding his hands beneath the material of both garments, he peeled them slowly back, enjoying the sight of her bare breasts coming into view. The cooler air made the dark peaks pucker in protest. He lowered his head and warmed her flesh with his breath, then his kisses. She tasted of fresh air and sunshine. She tasted like his Emily.

Kat's breath on her skin sent waves of desire coursing through Emily stronger than anything she'd felt when she was with him. She consciously pushed all thought of Rose and her secret far from her mind and opened it only to the sensations of Kat loving her.

How had she lived without his sweet persuasion in her life, without his touch, his kisses? In the last few weeks, since his return, he had become her life-blood, her anchor, her—

The tickle of the grass against her bare back brought her alert enough to realize that somehow Kat had removed her blouse and was about to slip her jeans shorts over her hips.

Closing her eyes, she surrendered to the sensations of pleasure his hands generated and his lips magnified.

One more time, she told herself. *Just one more time.* Then she'd distance herself. Until then—

Chapter Thirteen

Emily's eyes jerked open.

The meadow had grown ominously quiet. Suddenly, it exploded with the sounds of life intruding on the intimate nest she and Kat had found. A bird squawked and flew from the oak sheltering them to seek cover. Seconds later, a stiff wind raked through the trees, ripping fragile leaves from the branches and tossing them over her and Kat's entwined bodies. In the distance, thunder rumbled, a warning that the dark clouds obscuring the sun promised more than just a darkening of the landscape.

As if the changes forecast the future for Emily, she shoved at Kat's shoulders.

"*No!*"

Emily pushed away from him, then rolled to her side, struggling to replace her clothing as she gained her feet.

"Em?"

She couldn't keep opening herself up to more hurt. Each time they made love, she grew closer to him, trusted him more, and each time she knew the pain of parting would cut deeper. She had to stop it now while she still could, while at least part of her heart was still salvageable.

Kat reached for her, his eyes reflecting things she didn't want to see. "Em, what is it? Did I hurt you?"

She paused. Her heart raced. Her mind raced in all directions. Her skin still tingled from his touch. And oh, how she wanted to throw herself back in the shelter of his arms. But she couldn't. Not if she wanted to survive emotionally. Unable to stop herself, she glanced at him.

Turning away, she ran as fast as she could, putting distance between herself and the look on his face. The same look that must have been there when he'd found his mother had abandoned him.

She nearly turned to tell him the secret that lay hidden in her heart, Rose's secret. But she didn't, because she couldn't. She'd promised Rose, and a promise was a promise. But why did keeping it have to hurt everyone it touched?

EMILY STARED DOWN at the rectangular plastic test wand on the edge of the white porcelain bathroom sink. A pink minus sign glared back at her.

Damn!

She had to be pregnant. She just *had* to be. Avoiding Kat was getting harder and harder. But not nearly as hard as trying to stop loving him.

After the episode of nearly making love in the meadow a week ago, she wasn't sure how much longer she could hang on and still ride this emotional roller coaster her life had turned into.

She wanted Kat with every nerve and fiber in her body, and even when he'd moved back into the spare room, the yearning hadn't stopped. If anything, it had gotten worse. She missed him lying beside her, missed waking up in his arms, finding comfort in his strength when life hit the bumpy spots. But she had to learn to get used to his absence. She had to.

She glanced down at the pregnancy test stick. This was the third time this week she'd done the test, and she refused to accept the minus as conclusive. What could she be doing wrong?

Closing her eyes, she repeated the instructions the druggist had given her.

"Drop urine on the test area, wait ten minutes and then watch for the color change indicating plus or minus."

She'd done exactly what he'd told her. Could he have left something out?

Dropping to her knees on the bathroom floor, she pulled the trash container from under the sink and began to paw through it. At last she found the directions.

Sitting on the closed toilet seat, she read them. Well, hells bells, he hadn't said anything about waiting until *after* she was scheduled to menstruate. That must be the problem. She could still be pregnant. It was just too early to detect it yet. Another week before she'd know for sure one way or the other.

That would take her very close to the deadline the codicil had given her.

Familiar waves of regret that a baby would give Kat the excuse he needed to drop out of her life again followed quickly on the heels of the elation of a possible pregnancy. She knew she should be glad that he'd soon be out of her life, and she was. Then again she wasn't.

"Oh, hell, I don't know what I want anymore," she told her reflection in the medicine cabinet mirror.

What with the possibility of losing Kat, her home and the chance to have the child she wanted so much, combined with the burden of carrying the secret she shared with Rose, she felt like she was being pulled in twenty directions at once.

Waves of confusion, indecision and frustration rolled over her like a high tide searching out its level on an eroded beach. Her eyes burned. Her throat filled with unshed tears. What should she do?

Well, one thing she would *not* do was cry. However, saying she wouldn't and managing not to proved to be two entirely different things.

Burying her face in her hands, she let her emotions find expression in her tears. All the tension of the last few weeks poured from her in torrents.

"Emily? Emily, is that you, dear? Are you all right?"

Rose!

She couldn't let her find her like this. Rose would ask too many questions, questions she'd expect Emily to supply answers to.

She looked around at the scattered evidence of the pregnancy test. Quickly, she scooped it into the white pharmacy bag and tucked it in the trash below an empty toothpaste box.

"Emily? Answer me."

"Yes, Rose, it's me. I'll be out in a second." Frantically, she tore off a few sheets of toilet tissue, wiped the evidence of her emotional outburst from her cheeks, then blew her nose.

"Are you crying?"

Emily swallowed. "No. Why would you think that?"

"Because your voice sounds funny."

"I...uh..." Her gaze fell on a bottle of mouthwash on the vanity. "I just choked on some mouthwash. I'm fine."

"Then, please open the door so I can put these towels away."

She quickly inspected her face in the medicine cabinet mirror. Angry red splotches ringed her swollen eyes. If she opened the door and faced Rose, she'd have to explain why choking on mouthwash made her looked like she'd just sobbed her heart out.

"Just leave them out there, Rose. I'll put them away when I'm through."

Silence. "Very well."

Her ear to the door, Emily waited for the sound of Rose's footsteps retreating down the hall. Convinced it was safe, she opened the door and reached for the neat stack of pink towels. A gentle hand closed around her wrist.

"Rose!"

"Yes, *Rose*." Her housekeeper surveyed Emily's swollen eyes. "Choked, huh?" She frowned at her. "That's it. I've kept my silence as long as a body can be expected to. Emily Madison, we need to have a little talk. I will expect you in the kitchen in five minutes. No excuses."

Rose stalked down the hall, the empty plastic clothes basket clutched so tightly against her body that it bent in the middle. Emily hadn't heard Rose use that commanding tone since, at seventeen, she'd stayed out with a friend until well after midnight and Rose had caught her sneaking in. Back then, Rose had accepted nothing but the truth. Emily had a strong suspicion that this was another of those times.

As EMILY WALKED into the kitchen, Kat noted her anxious expression. When Chuck had come to get him, telling him Rose wanted him at the house as soon as possible, he'd rushed back thinking something was wrong with Emily. As soon as he'd stepped through the door, Rose had ambushed him, told him to sit, and that as soon as Emily got there, the three of them would be having a talk.

He could tell by the tone of Rose's voice and the look of resignation on his wife's face that this was not going to be a pleasant chat over coffee. Something was up. He wondered if it had anything to do with him moving back to the spare room. He was sure Rose had noticed. How could she not? After all, she changed the sheets, she had to know someone was sleeping in the extra room. Realistically, he'd known he'd end up explaining it to the sharp-eyed housekeeper, but he'd found the prospect of facing Rose preferable to enduring another night beside Emily without touching her.

Emily slipped into the chair at the end of the table. Far enough from him, he noted painfully, that they wouldn't touch, even accidentally. Rose finished pouring coffee, transferred three cups, a cream pitcher and a sugar bowl to the table, then she sat.

Folding her hands in front of her, she waited. The smell of the freshly brewed coffee filled the air, along with that of the chocolate cake Rose had set on the counter to cool before icing.

"Well, which one of you is going to tell me what in blazes is going on?" Rose's tone allowed no room for evasions.

He'd been right. This was not going to be one of their friendly coffee klatches. He trained his attention on Emily. As if feeling his gaze, she glanced up at him from beneath lowered lashes. Her eyes were red. She'd been crying. Why? Had she and Rose had an argument?

Impatient to get this over with, Kat opened the conversation. "Rose, what's the problem here?" While waiting for Rose's reply, he kept a vigilant eye on Emily, who looked fragile enough to pass out at any moment. Her spoon clanked noisily against her saucer.

Rose turned a questioning expression on Emily. "That's what I want to know." She looked back to Kat. "I've been watching the two of you, and I can't figure out what's going on." She stirred sugar into her black coffee. "First you move into the spare room, then I find her crying in the bathroom. And I don't need a degree in rocket science to see the way she's been avoiding you all week.'' She glared from one to the other. ''Your actions all week are certainly not those of two people who are supposed to be in love.''

''We're just—''

Emily spoke up. ''No, Kat. Let me. It's my fault that this mess started to begin with. Besides, I'm tired of the subterfuge and it's time Rose knew the truth.''

Rose looked to Emily expectantly. ''The truth?''

Placing the spoon she'd been fingering on the flowered placemat, Emily cleared her throat. ''Kat and I got married to have a child.''

A smile broke out on Rose's lips. ''Well, is that all—''

''There's more.'' Emily paused, her expression giving away her fight to find the words to finish. ''Lawrence Tippens called me to his office a week after you left for Mexico. He said he'd only just found out that if I didn't have a baby, I would lose the farm. So, I asked Kat to father it. He agreed, but only if we were married.'' She sent a nervous glance at Kat, then lowered her gaze to her cup. ''We're not…. There's no other reason.''

''That damned codicil.'' Though Rose mumbled the words, Emily heard them.

''You knew about the codicil?'' Emily's mouth hung open. She couldn't believe Rose had known and never said anything.

Pushing aside her coffee cup, Rose nodded. ''Yes,

I knew. Why do you think I went out of my way to introduce you to so many young men? Not that it did any good. Your father told me about it right after he went to the lawyer's to have it drawn up. I tried to talk him out of it, but he wouldn't listen.'' She raised her gaze to Emily's. "You know your father when he got a bee in his bonnet.''

Emily didn't move a muscle. Yes, she'd known her father, and she thought she'd known Rose. "Why didn't you tell me?"

"Because I promised Frank I wouldn't.''

"But why would he ask for a promise like that?"

Rose took Emily's hand, but Emily pulled away. "Because he knew how you felt about this place and he wanted you to find love, not just to run off and marry anyone to keep the farm.''

Mirthless laughter broke from Emily. "How ironic, seeing as how that's exactly what I did.'' *In both cases,* she added silently.

"I thought you knew about the codicil and were just dragging your feet. I don't understand why the lawyer waited so long to tell you. It was supposed to be read along with Frank's will.'' Rose shook her head. "He said you'd know well in advance of your thirtieth birthday.''

When Emily couldn't find the words to explain how fate had twisted her life into a corkscrew, Kat spoke up. "The codicil got lost. They just ran across it while you were in Mexico. Emily asked me to help her and I agreed because we've been friends for so long.''

Rose looked from one to the other. "You mean you two aren't...you're just...."

"We're not in love, if that's what you're asking," Kat supplied. "Are we, Emily?"

She could feel his dark gaze boring into her, waiting for an answer. Unable to voice the lie or meet his gaze, she just shook her head and kept her eyes focused on her coffee cup.

"That's what I thought," he said.

A chair scraped across the floor. She looked up in time to see Kat going out the back door.

Rose shook her head. "Some men just can't see what's sitting right in front of them." For a long moment, she stared at the closed door, then turned back to Emily. She studied her for another few moments, then shrugged. "Your dad meant well, child."

Her words roused Emily. "Meant well? He's messed up my entire life, and all you can say is he meant well?" She raised her face and looked at the woman she'd loved like a mother, the woman who had known about this codicil and never told her. "Do you have any idea the hurt this has caused? Why didn't you tell me?"

"I should have. I can see that now. I knew back then that no good would come of this." She frowned, then scooted her chair close enough to Emily to grab her hand. "Emily, listen to me. Your father loved you." A squeeze to Emily's hand emphasized each word. "He knew you loved this farm, but he didn't want to see you end up like he did."

"Like he did?"

"Lonely, bitter, alone."

She didn't understand. Her father had been one of the most self-sufficient men she'd ever known, needing no one, wanting nothing from anyone, least of all love from his three children.

"I know. You think of Frank as cold and heartless, don't you?"

Emily nodded, still too stunned by Rose's words to speak.

"He wasn't. He was a man who lived every day of his life with the pain the of losing the only woman he truly loved."

"But my mother's death never seemed to bother him that much." She recalled him going about his life after the funeral as if nothing had happened, playing poker on Friday night with the other local breeders, going to the Horseman's Club for his usual nightly gossip session and drinks with his friends. If he'd been so devastated about her mother's death, he certainly had put on a good front.

"Not *your* mother, child. Jesse's mother. He never forgave her for leaving him and taking his son, but he loved that woman with every breath, right up until the day she died." She patted Emily's hand. "That's why he never could show his love for Jesse. The poor boy couldn't help that he looked exactly like his mother, but even though he loved Jesse, Frank saw him as a constant reminder of her desertion."

"How do you know all this?" Her father, to Emily's knowledge, had never told anyone about his first wife. In fact, until Jesse showed up on their doorstep holding the hand of a social worker and carrying one battered suitcase, Honey and she had always assumed that their mother was the only wife Frank had ever had.

Rose released Emily's hand and leaned back in her chair. "I found him one night, him and what was left of a bottle of Scotch. He told me it was the anniversary of his first marriage. Puzzled, I asked him what he meant. Then he told me." She shook her head. A strand of hair fell over her forehead. She swept it back. "I should have told you. But I'd promised. You of all people should understand that."

Oh, she understood. But she also knew her father had said that certain promises were made to be broken. Until right this moment, she hadn't understood that. She'd always believed that it was just his way of excusing what he did. Because of his careless lack of consideration for others, she'd believed all promises were sacred, that once given, they should never be revoked or broken.

Now that she knew her father's reasoning, the mess that had resulted from his decision to interfere in her life seemed even more ironic. He'd tried to ensure her happiness and had, instead, turned her life to chaos and ensured her unhappiness. How could her father have known that she'd end up falling in love with Kat?

Rose cleared away the coffee cups and took them to the sink. She leaned on the edge and looked out the window. "It's amazing how much heartache a body can cause by doing what they think is right. First my own son, then you.''

Kat!

Her own problems disappeared. Another promise, the promise she'd made to Rose, invaded her thoughts.

Was this one of those promises that were made to be broken, one of those promises that ends up hurting people if it's honored? A promise like the one her father had asked Rose to make? Did Emily have the right to break her promise to Rose merely because she thought Kat should know? Did that give her the right to forsake her word?

Emily had never broken a promise in her life. Would this one be the first?

"WELL, LITTLE SISTER, I'd say that by prying into Rose's personal life, you brought this on yourself." Honey wound the cord around the brackets on the vacuum cleaner, then placed it in the broom closet and closed the door. She eyed Emily across the large pantry. "Are you sure you don't want to tell me what this monumental secret is?"

Emily shook her head. "I can't, Honey. I promised Rose."

"I'm sorry. That wasn't fair." Taking Emily's arm, she led her through the downstairs of the house. "I need to look for something to wear to Danny's nursery school play. Come help me decide."

They climbed the long open staircase to the second floor in silence. Settled on the edge of Honey's bed, Emily tried to act interested in the parade of garments Honey wanted opinions on. But the interest just wasn't there.

"Well, you've been a huge help," Honey said, placing the last of the dresses she'd pulled out of the vast wardrobe on a chair. She sat next to Emily. "You've always put too much emphasis on promises, Em. It's time you started looking at them realistically. Sometimes we make promises to ourselves and others and then wish we hadn't." Honey hugged her sister briefly. "Only you can make the decision as to whether or not to keep Rose's secret." Standing, she walked to the window and drew back the curtain.

This time, Emily didn't think Honey was checking on Danny. Her gaze had turned toward the overcast sky, a dreamy expression on her face. Since Honey seldom took too much of life seriously—with the exception of raising her son—Emily's attention was riveted on her sister.

Rain began to fall in soft drops against the window. Honey traced the journey of one drop with the tip of her finger.

"Sometimes promises you refuse to break change your life. Change the lives of those around you. Hurt people who don't deserve to be hurt." She sighed and dropped the curtain. "Too late you realize that the promise you made was never meant to be made. That the information you're holding back should have been told. That you didn't have the right to decide whether or not to keep the promise."

A gut feeling told Emily that Honey was no longer talking about the promise to Rose. "Honey?"

Her sister swung away from the window, an embarrassed smile curving her lips. "I'm sorry. Got a bit carried away there." Wiping the moisture from her hands on the legs of her faded jeans, she picked up a green dress from the pile on the boudoir chair. "So, what do you think of this one? Think I'll look motherly in it? Danny already warned me not to wear anything too sexy." She laughed. "Tell me what a four-year-old kid knows from sexy?" She glanced at Emily and held out the dress. "So, what do you think?"

"It's fine."

The dress could have been a potato sack for all Emily knew. She was still busy trying to digest what Honey had just said. "So, you're saying that if this promise will end up hurting people if I don't divulge it, then I should tell?"

Honey stepped in front of the cheval mirror, the dress plastered against her front. Surveying the effect, she locked gazes with Emily. The dress fell to the floor. She took a seat beside Emily. "I'm saying that only you can make that call. Only you know how breaking your promise will affect the people involved. Go with your heart, Em."

Honey was right. Emily had been worried about her own ethics. What she should have been worrying about was the people she loved being hurt by her silence. She'd follow her heart and her heart urged her to tell Kat about Rose.

Chapter Fourteen

Toolbox in hand, Kat raced toward the house, trying to outrun the impending storm. As he rounded the corner of the barn, he noted that both Emily's car and Rose's were missing. Only his blue truck stood in the driveway.

Just as his foot hit the top step, the ominous clouds opened and rain began to fall, first in soft drops, then harder, in pounding torrents that quickly produced a wash of water running off the eaves of the porch. He studied the horizon above the mountains to the north. The clouds stretched on in a never-ending cap of gray. He could forget about getting any more done on the house today. By the time the rain stopped, it would be too dark to work.

However, the emotions that had driven him from the house when Emily had admitted there was no love in their relationship, now drove him with an excess of angry energy that needed to find an outlet. If he had to sit alone in the house thinking about what he couldn't have, he'd go nuts.

As he walked through the kitchen door, then

slipped off his work boots on the rag rug Rose had provided for muddy shoes, he noticed her to-do list secured to the front of the refrigerator by a ceramic, yellow carnation magnet. No time like the present to make a dent in the list, and the fix-it chores were just the thing he needed to work out the kinks in his tight nerves.

Using a paper towel, he wiped the mud from the bottom of his toolbox. Rose would skin him alive if he tracked mud through her clean house. As he worked, he thought about Rose and her relationship with Emily. It reminded him of his mother's relationship with him. He corrected that to *adoptive* mother.

Oh hell, what difference did a word make? Hilda Madison had been more of a mother to him than blood could have made her. She'd loved him, cared for him and always been there for him. Which was a hell of a lot more than his biological mother had done.

He halted those thoughts. They'd get him nowhere. He had to put all that from his mind.

Picking up the toolbox, he grabbed an apple from the fruit bowl on the counter, then headed toward the hall and upstairs to fix Rose's bedroom closet door. The sweetness of the crisp apple reminded him of the days when he and Emily raided Old Man Watkin's apple orchard, then made themselves sick trying to eat up the evidence of their crime.

He stopped chewing and dumped the half-eaten apple in the trash.

The flimsy curtains let only the storm-darkened

daylight into Rose's room. He flipped on the light, then walked to the closet door. He swung it toward him. It stopped half open. From the depths of the closet came the scent of her perfume—lily of the valley. He smiled.

Looking around for somewhere to sit his toolbox that would be convenient, yet high enough for him to easily reach his tools, he decided on her dresser. Pushing aside the items neatly lined up on the white lace doily to protect the dark mahogany surface, he reached for the toolbox, but stopped suddenly.

Straightening, he walked closer to the dresser. Positioned in the center, beneath the mirror, was a wooden box. Hesitantly, as if it would burn him, he reached for it. Instead of picking it up, he ran his fingertip over the design in the lid. His insides burned with recognition of the rose and heart, the same rose and heart that were carved into the foot of the cradle in his room.

Afraid that he was imagining things, he retrieved the cradle, set it on the rug, then placed the wooden box beside it. There was no doubt that the two had been carved by the same hand. He could do little more than stare at his find. His mind worked frantically to assimilate what it could mean. Why did Rose have this box? Where had she gotten it?

From somewhere outside the realm of clear comprehension, the sound of a car in the driveway and then, moments later, the front door opening and closing threatened to penetrate the fog of emotions enveloping him. But he wouldn't allow any other thoughts admittance. He had to figure this out.

Did Rose know who had carved the box and cradle? Did she hold the key to his biological parents' identity? Was that the reason for her odd scrutiny of him? Her reaction the day she'd seen him polishing the cradle?

Questions and more questions stampeded through his mind.

"Oh, my God!"

Rose's voice brought his head up sharply. She stood in the doorway, her hand covering her mouth. Her blue eyes, wide and terrified, darted from Kat to the wooden items beside him, then back to Kat. Her other hand clutched the doorframe, as if, should she let go, her legs would give way.

He pointed to the box and cradle. "Where did these things come from?"

For a long time, she didn't answer. Kat had to physically hold himself back from shaking the answers from her. Finally she dropped her hand and took a seat on the bed. At first she stared at the floor, then she raised her tear-filled gaze to his.

"My father had them made for me."

"Your—" The answer he'd hoped would clear up his questions instead gave birth to more. "How? I mean the cradle—"

"The cradle was a gift from him, when he found out I was pregnant with his grandson." Her voice was barely audible above the rush of rain hitting the windowpane.

"His—" The thoughts taking form in Kat's mind bordered on unbelievable. He had to be wrong. Things like this only happened in movies and books.

Still, he had to ask, just to know. "Who are you?"

His question seemed to make Rose's tears flow faster. As she reached for a tissue, her hands shook so badly she could barely pull it from the box. She wiped at her wet cheeks, then blew her nose. Throwing the tissue into the wastebasket, she straightened her spine, as if preparing to go into battle. Then she stood and faced him squarely, her chin elevated slightly.

"I'm your mother."

The breath left Kat's lungs in one gust of air. He felt as if he'd been kicked in the gut. Struggling for a center, he put out his hand for something solid. Feeling the smooth wood of the dresser beneath his palm, he leaned into the edge. The bite of the wood in his hip helped him come back to the reality of the moment.

"I know this is a shock," Rose was saying, her hand extended imploringly toward him.

She took a step in his direction. He recoiled, shoving the corner of the dresser deeper into his hip. The pain felt good compared to the pain slicing its way through his heart.

"I'm sorry."

"Sorry?" He barely recognized his own voice. "Sorry? That's supposed to take care of everything? Of years of looking for you, of days and nights of wondering, of—"

"No. I know that sorry isn't enough. I know that I can never excuse what I did, but you must let me tell you—"

"I don't want to hear it." His growled statement

surprised him almost as much as it did Rose. ''I don't want your excuses.''

All these years. All this time. All he'd ever wanted was for someone to tell him *why*. But standing here, looking into her face, he realized that nothing could excuse what she'd done. Not enough words existed in the English language to explain away abandoning your child.

''I will never forgive you,'' he ground out.

Pushing past her, he stormed from the room. Closing his ears to her heart-wrenching sobs, to her tearful pleas to come back, he walked blindly away from the mother he'd worked so hard to find.

PARKING IN THE YARD, Emily's gaze followed the path of light her high beams cast on the old house. In the swath of light, she could see all the way to the roof eaves. How she'd once loved this place. In the last few weeks, she'd come to realize that nails, wood, brick and mortar were no substitute for the real things that made a house a home—loving and being loved, sharing it with those you love.

The figure of a man running toward the Madison house caught her attention. Between the swipe of the windshield wipers, she realized it was Kat. The only light in her house shone from the upstairs bedroom window where Rose watched Kat's progress across the rain-soaked grass.

Emily's heart twisted for Rose's pain. To keep from causing her son more heartache, she was willing to stand on the outside of his life, catching glimpses of him through a window.

Torn between going to Rose and to Kat, she sat in the car, engulfed in guilt, helpless to aid either of them. For a long time, she simply stared out the windshield, acutely aware that, if she broke her promise to Rose and told Kat about his mother, she had it in her power to bring both of them peace or disrupt their lives forever. Which would it be? Her heart answered for her.

She could talk to Rose later. Right now she needed to get to Kat and tell him Rose's secret and hope that he'd understand. Opening the car door, she hunched her shoulders against the cold rain, stepped out and then slammed the door.

Running, she headed for the Madison house. She hadn't a clue what she'd say to Kat, just that she'd tell him the truth.

Inside the house, she wound her way through the dark, familiar rooms, looking for him. In the room that had been his parents', she found him sitting on the floor, his gaze centered somewhere outside the rain-washed window.

"Kat, there's something I have to tell you."

He didn't acknowledge her presence with as much as a flicker of an eyelash.

The rain had stopped and the clouds were clearing from the sky. The moon shed weak beams of milky light through the dirty window, enough for her to see his face. His expression made her hesitate. Firming her resolve, she walked slowly toward him, her heart breaking at his look of pain. Suddenly, in her heart, she knew she was too late. He'd already found out who Rose was. Nothing remained for her to do except try to make him see why Rose had left him.

"Kat, let me explain about Rose and why she did it."

He turned to her, the pain in his face replaced with a mask of anger. "You knew?"

She nodded.

"How could you do this, Emily? You of all people. You knew how important this was to me."

The look of betrayal he flashed at her left her speechless. She'd never seen Kat look like this before. So hard. So unforgiving. As if he truly hated her. That hurt more than anything he could have said, any reprimand, any anger, anything.

"I promised not to say anything."

"And heaven forbid you should break a promise, right?" His tone cut deep.

What he thought of her and her ethics didn't matter. Making Kat see that he was hurting Rose and himself was too important.

"Kat, she loves you. What she did, she did because—"

He bounded to his feet and faced her. "No! I didn't want to hear it from her and I certainly don't want to hear it from you."

"But—"

"No, Emily!" In the anemic moonlight, his dark eyes took on a feral quality. "Don't you see? As much as I wanted to know why she walked out on me is as much as it no longer matters. She did and that's the bottom line."

Emily laid her hand on his forearm. "No, it's

not.'' She kept her voice controlled and soft, hoping not to fuel his anger. ''The bottom line is that when you love someone, you'll do whatever it takes to ensure their happiness and well-being, no matter how much it hurts you to do it, no matter how much your heart cries for it to be otherwise. All she did, Kat, was love you.'' She swallowed her own pain. ''Do you have any idea how much strength it takes to love someone, then let them go because it's what's best for them?''

Emily knew, deep inside, she wasn't talking only to Kat, but to herself as well.

''What do you know about love? You've managed to keep yourself a safe distance from that emotion all your life.''

His words slashed through her. What could she say? That she knew love could be a blissful trip to the stars or a plunging ride into hell? That loving someone with everything in you didn't mean they'd love you back? In the end, she said nothing.

He tore his heated gaze from her, then turned away, his shoulders tight and stiff, visual proof of his unbending attitude. He began pacing the length of the room. ''Why did I ever come back to this place?''

''A better question is, why did you stay?'' She waited breathlessly, hoping.

''Because I was too stupid to see that there's nothing here for me, never was.'' He stalked toward the door. ''But I've smartened up, Em.''

She watched him walk from the room, her heart crying out to him to come back, but she said nothing. A silly poem she'd heard once about loving someone and setting them free and if they loved you, they would come back, played through her mind.

From the window she watched him climb into his truck and pull out of the driveway. She watched the truck go down the road. She watched until her tears blotted out everything but the blur of red taillights fading into the night.

THE FOLLOWING MORNING, after an endless night of tossing and turning, Emily rolled to her side, then reached groggily for the ringing phone.

"Hellum."

"Emily?"

"Yes." Who was this idiot calling her at—she glanced at the red digital numbers on her alarm clock—eight o'clock in the morning? "Who is this?"

"Lawrence Tippens."

Great! Just what she needed right now, a long chat with Perry Mason. "Yes, Larry? I hope you're not calling to tell me you just discovered another codicil that requires I climb Mount Everest in the nude."

She wasn't sure if his indignant gasp came from the use of his nickname or her risqué statement, but whichever it was, it gave her a perverse pleasure to make him uncomfortable.

"Nothing like that." He cleared his throat. "I'm calling to see if…well, to see if you've…well, if—"

"No. I'm not pregnant, Larry, if that's what

you're trying to ask.'' Lord deliver her from a prudish male.

''Then it's my duty to inform you that your time will have elapsed in a week.''

Anger seeped through her. She didn't give a damn about the farm. Emily sat up as if propelled by a spring. The room swam before her. Quickly, she lay back down. Blinking to clear her head, she waited for the nausea that accompanied the dizziness to pass.

''Emily? Are you still there?''

''Yes.'' Her tone came across more sharply than she'd intended. ''I'm still here.''

''Unless some biological adjustment to your body becomes apparent, I'm afraid I'll have to enforce the terms of the codicil.''

Biological adjustment? They were discussing a flesh-and-blood child, not the formation of some disease. ''Do what you have to do, Larry.'' She hung up.

Cautiously, she eased herself into a sitting position. She really didn't need to get sick right now, not with Rose and Kat to contend with.

Well, Emily, that's what running around in the rain trying to convince some pig-headed man that he's got his head on backwards will do for you.

But her sarcastic wall of defense couldn't erase the rush of loneliness she felt, knowing Kat could well be out of her life forever. That she might never see Kat again sent a sharp pain to her very soul.

She rubbed at her gritty eyes with the heels of her hands. Right now, she had to get up and see about

Rose. By the time she'd come back to the house the night before, Rose had been asleep, or at least that's what Emily was led to believe when she'd tapped softly on the bedroom door and got no answer.

Pushing the covers back, she eased her feet to the floor. Her head seemed fine. Her throat wasn't sore. Exactly what had that dizzy thing been? She'd think about it later. Right now, she had other things to take care of.

Grabbing her robe, she padded down the hall to Rose's room, then knocked softly. The door swung open by itself. She stopped.

Next to the bed, Rose folded a blue flowered dress, then neatly added it to the suitcase stretched open on the coverlet.

Panic and confusion gripped Emily in an icy hand. "What's going on?"

The older woman smiled sadly. "I'm leaving."

Chapter Fifteen

"You can't leave, not now." Emily moved into Rose's bedroom and stood beside her.

Rose glanced at Emily, shook her head, then began removing the contents of the top dresser drawer. "Kat knows who I am and I can't stay. I can't bear to see the hate in my son's eyes every day. I just can't."

Emily flopped down beside the suitcase on the bed. Absently, she fingered the holes in the white lace coverlet. How could she tell Rose that Kat had left? She had to. There was no getting around it. She'd find out sooner or later. "He's not going to be here."

"What?" Rose's movements froze. The undergarments meant for the suitcase hung from her hand as she stared at Emily. "I don't understand."

"He's gone, Rose. Left last night."

"Gone? Where?"

Emily shrugged.

Rose collapsed beside her. "He's gone because of me."

No sense trying to sugarcoat it. Rose would see through it and that would serve no purpose. Emily took her housekeeper's hand. "That's only one of the reasons. I'm the other."

"But he loves you. Why would he leave you?"

The idea of Kat loving her brought choking tears to Emily's throat. "If only he did."

"But he does." Rose looked imploring at her daughter-in-law. "I've seen it in his eyes, child. No man looks at a woman like that without love in his heart." She smiled. "And this may come as a surprise to you, but you love him, too."

"No. It's no surprise. I've been in love with him for years. I just never knew it until he came back."

"You need to tell him."

To Emily's sorrow, Rose was right. She should have told him and begged him to stay. If she hadn't been afraid of his reaction, she would have. Rose's face blurred through Emily's tears. "It's got nothing to do with love either."

"Then, if it's not because of love, what made him leave?"

Emily held back. She didn't want to add any more guilt to the burden Rose already shouldered for Kat's leaving.

"Emily? Please be honest with me."

Rose might not deserve the guilt, but she did deserve the honesty. "I told him I knew who you are, that I'd known for some time."

"And he was angry because you kept my secret from him?"

Looking down at her hands, Emily nodded. "I've

never seen him that angry." Tears burned her eyes. "So, you see, it's too late."

"It's never too late for love. He'll come back. Right now, he's hurt. He needs time to forgive you."

"And you?"

Picking up the undergarments she'd put aside, Rose stood. "That's another story. What I did to him can't be forgiven. I realized that when I saw the look on his face."

Emily stopped her from placing the garments in the suitcase. "You're wrong. I've seen the two of you chatting and joking over a cup of coffee. Kat has grown to love you. That's not something he can turn off." She stood. "Give him that chance. If he comes back here, it won't be because of me." In her heart, she knew he would never forgive her for not breaking her promise to Rose. "He'll come back for his mother."

KAT SIPPED the terrible black brew he'd made every morning for the last week and called coffee. Even Emily's wasn't this bad. He leaned back on the sofa and looked around the sparsely furnished summer cottage. A far cry from the cozy living room at Clover Hill Farms.

Thank goodness he'd never told Dave Thornton he didn't need the house he'd arranged for him. A small town like Bristol didn't have motels. The night he'd stormed out of the Madison house, he'd been in no mood to drive far. He could be comfortable here until he sold the house. It had everything he needed—

His thoughts took a sharp turn toward the one thing he needed that the cottage didn't have, would never have. Emily. Emily, his lifeline, his friend, the woman he loved. The woman who'd betrayed him.

Now that he'd calmed down and could think sanely about it, he knew that he'd been wrong to take his anger at Rose out on Em. She'd always had strong ethics. He'd been aware of them since childhood.

It shouldn't have shocked him that she still had them. Because of her life with Frank Kingston, promises meant more to her than the average person. Was it any wonder that she had kept the one she'd made to Rose?

For the thousandth time, the scene between him and Em played out in his mind. Her voice. Her pleas. Her—

He sat up straighter. When Emily had come into the room, she'd said she had something to tell him. And seconds later, she hadn't denied knowing Rose's identity. She'd known and had been ready to tell him, ready to break a promise for him.

When he thought about the hurtful words he'd thrown at her, he could cut out his tongue. It wasn't her fault she couldn't return his love. His heart twisted with the pain of remembering the look in her eyes when he'd said he didn't know why he'd come back, and she'd asked why he'd stayed. That look of…had it been hope? Hope that he loved her?

Had he been wrong? His heart began to beat faster. *Did* Emily love him? Was he reading things into a look? Had he been fair to her by just brushing her off and storming out, running away?

Then he recalled the passionate woman he'd made love to. The woman who'd clung to him, reaching heights of urgency that he'd never seen in a woman before. He recalled the hope in her eyes. The hope he'd destroyed with his careless words.

And while he was thinking about fair, how about Rose? He'd never given her a chance to explain anything. He'd just drawn his own conclusions and stalked off.

If he wanted to be honest with himself, he'd been running from things in one way or another for the past sixteen years. It was about time he stopped.

The first step in that direction was to go see both Emily and Rose and hope he hadn't done any irreparable damage.

First, he had to make a couple of phone calls. He reached for the phone.

Twenty minutes later, a smile of satisfaction painting his lips, he grabbed his truck keys off the end table and headed toward the door.

A WEEK HAD PASSED since Emily had succeeded in talking Rose into staying at least until she could hire another housekeeper. She figured if she dragged her feet long enough, Rose would change her mind. However, Emily had not failed to notice that Rose had not unpacked her suitcase.

That thought, the little bit of sleep she'd gotten since Kat had left and this nagging feeling of impending nausea did little to stop her head from throbbing. For that matter, the smell of the French toast Rose was making for her only made her stomach churn more.

The day had taken a downward spiral when Larry Tippens had called again to smugly tell her the time was up and the farm had been signed over to the Horseman's Benevolent Association. She supposed he'd thought she'd feel better when he'd added, with a pleased smile in his voice, that the Association had already found a buyer for the farm. She had till the end of the month before the new owner took possession. Probably her payback for all the times she'd refused to go out with Lawrence in high school.

It must have been very disappointing to him when she didn't get upset. The farm didn't matter anymore, now that Kat wasn't there to share it with her and Rose was planning to leave. Everything and everyone she'd loved most was either going or gone.

Just the thought made her upset stomach churn harder.

"Here you are." Rose set a plate of French toast and bacon in front of her. "I want to see you eat all of that. You've been looking peaked lately."

To make sure she did, she noted that Rose got her coffee and sat down across from her. The smell of cinnamon and grease drifted up to her. She swallowed hard several times. Hoping it would help, she took a sip of coffee. Her stomach heaved.

Slamming her hand over her mouth, she dashed for the downstairs bathroom.

Minutes later, she emerged. Having checked the

mirror, Emily knew her face bore the ravages of her recent bathroom trip. She felt as if someone had wrung her out and hung her up to dry. Pushing the plate of French toast to the far side of the table, she collapsed in the chair.

"My goodness, you look like death warmed over," Rose exclaimed.

"It's this darn stomach virus. I haven't been able to shake it all week." Rose was studying her with a sly smile. "What?"

"I'm thinking it's not a stomach virus."

"Of course it is. What else could it be?"

Rose said nothing. She just continued to stare at Emily with one eyebrow lifted in question. Suddenly, what Rose was trying to tell her registered. She'd been so preoccupied with everything else going on, she'd forgotten all about the baby.

"You don't think that…that I…that there's…" No matter how she tried, she could not force either the word *baby* or the word *pregnant* off her tongue.

Grinning, Rose nodded. "That's exactly what I think."

Dragging her tired, weak body to her feet, Emily shuffled to the counter, then pulled her pocket calendar from her purse. Nervously, she fumbled through the pages to the right month. With the tip of her finger, she followed the line of Xs in the boxes. According to this, her period was over a week late. She was going to have a baby—Kat's baby.

Happiness bubbled within her, but with it came

deep heartache. "How ironic," she whispered, fighting back new tears. "What am I going to do?"

"Well, I know what I'm going to do." Rose came up behind Emily and squeezed her bent shoulders. "I deserted one baby in my lifetime. I don't plan on deserting another, especially not my grandchild. I'll just go up and unpack."

TWO DAYS LATER, Kat pulled his truck into the driveway and parked between Emily's and Rose's cars. He took a deep breath and looked at the house.

"Well, you're here. Sitting in the car like a coward isn't going to get you anywhere."

Resolutely, he opened the door and unfolded his body from the vehicle. He hitched up his jeans and walked toward his fate.

The open back door allowed the smell of fresh-baked cookies to drift out to meet him. Rose was in the kitchen. With her back to him taking a sheet of cookies from the oven, she didn't even hear him come in. When she turned, she let out a gasp and dropped the cookie sheet. It clattered to the tile floor. Chocolate chip cookies rolled about at her feet, but she didn't notice. Her gaze was riveted on him.

"Hi," he offered lamely.

Only then did she seem to rouse from shock and look down. "Now, look at this," she said, squatting to gather the cookies.

"Let me help." He hurried to her side and took the cookies from her. Their gazes locked.

Funny, but he'd never noticed the color of her eyes before or the way little laugh lines spread out in fans from the corners of them. He'd never seen the kindness in her face before, at least not the way he did now. She wet her lips with her tongue, something he always did when he was nervous. Something he did now.

"I'd like to talk to you, if you don't mind."

They stood together.

"I don't mind." She fidgeted with the hem of her apron, wringing it between her hands. "Would you like some coffee?"

He grinned. "I told you before I never pass up coffee with a beautiful woman."

She stared at him, as if seeing him for the first time, then flashed a weak, hesitant smile, as if she wasn't sure it was all right. He hated himself for making her feel that way. "I'll have some ready in a jiffy."

He took a seat and, with a new appreciation, watched Rose work. This was his mother, the woman who had given him life. *Then left you,* a tiny nuisance voice reminded him. He ignored it. "Where's Emily?"

"She's lying down. "She…uh…hasn't been feeling up to par lately."

"Em's sick?" Kat was on his feet and heading for the hall. Rose caught his arm and stopped him.

"She's fine. Just a bit tired."

If Em hadn't been getting any more sleep than he had lately, he could understand that. He went back to his seat at the table and divided his attention between his mother and the hall stairs.

"Are you sure she's okay?"

"Yes, I'm very sure."

Instead of joining him at the table while the coffee brewed, Rose busied herself cleaning up her baking mess, then putting some of the cool cookies on a plate. Just before the coffee pot gurgled for the last time, she moved the plate of cookies to the table. Another trip brought cups and spoons.

Kat knew she was putting off their talk as long as she could. He waited. He'd waited all these years, he could wait a bit longer.

Finally, when she could find no reason not to, Rose joined him at the table with the coffee pot. He waited until she'd poured the steaming brew into both cups and set the pot on a hot plate.

"I was very unfair to you when I found that box. I never let you explain." She looked down at her lap. "I'm ready to listen now, if you want to tell me what happened."

Rose faced him squarely, her eyes brimming with unshed tears. Then, she raised her chin, just as she'd done in her room that day, and began talking. An hour later, she looked at him again, with pleading in her eyes.

"Can you ever forgive me?"

He took her hand between his. "Someone we both love told me that it takes a lot of strength to love someone and let them go because you know it's best for them. Thanks to your unselfishness, I had a very good life, with people who loved me. I hardly think you need to be forgiven for that...Mom."

Tears flowed from Rose's eyes. Kat stood, drew

her up from her chair and enveloped her in his embrace.

"I never thought...never dared dream..."

"Shhh. As of today, we're putting the past behind us. No more might-have-beens or should-have-beens. Just tomorrow." He put her at arm's length. "Deal?"

She nodded. "Deal." She sniffed loudly, dug a tissue from her apron pocket, wiped her nose, then smiled at him. "Now, why don't you go see to that wife of yours? She has some crazy notion that you don't love her."

He returned her smile and started for the hall.

"Son?"

The word stopped him in his tracks. Loving warmth washed over him. He turned. "Yes?"

"I love you."

Tears filled his throat, preventing speech. He smiled and nodded, then turned back to the stairs.

EVER SINCE she'd heard the car come into the driveway, Emily had been drifting fitfully in and out of sleep. Dreams of Kat haunted her.

When she opened her eyes and found him standing over her, she thought it was just another dream. Not until he sat on the bed and she felt it gave under his weight would she believe that it was actually him.

"Hey, Squirt." He smiled.

Her heartbeat sped up. "Hey."

"You awake enough to talk?"

She nodded, fearful that if she spoke, he'd vanish.

He checked out her face, then frowned. "You feel okay?"

Again she nodded.

"You sure? Rose said you've been sick."

"Just an upset stomach. It usually goes away by midmorning, though."

"I want to talk to you about this deal we made."

Here it comes. He's going to tell me he's leaving. She couldn't bear to hear him say the words. Emily slid from the bed and cautiously stood. "There is no deal anymore. The time is up. I've lost the house. There's no reason for you to stay. But thanks for trying. When you sell your house, you're free to go."

"Em, I sold the house already."

Pain streaked through her. She'd counted on a few more days, just a few. "Well, then you have no ties to keep you here. You can leave whenever you want." She turned to him, an artificial smile plastered across her lips. "I'm happy for you."

In a flash, he was up off the bed and had her shoulders clamped between his large hands. "You know, if conclusion-jumping were an Olympic event, you'd be a gold medalist."

Stunned, she could only stare at him, trying to piece together what he was saying.

"I've spent half my life following your lead, just to make sure you didn't break your fool neck. This time you're going to listen to me and we're going to do things my way."

Before she could reply, he pulled her to him and covered her lips with his. Streaks of fire coursed through her body. It had been so long since Kat had kissed her, really kissed her. Her head spun and her nerves came alive. She wrapped her arms around his neck and held on, for fear he might still change his mind.

Kat gloried in her response. For a minute, until she'd returned his kiss, he'd thought he'd lost her. Now, he was sure Emily was his. He tightened his embrace and spun her in a wide circle. "Emily Kingston Madison, I love you."

Emily stiffened and pushed from him. She slapped her hand over her mouth and dashed for the bathroom. From outside, he could hear her being sick.

When there was silence again from the other side of the door, he called to her. "Emily, are you okay?"

"Fine." Her muffled reply only unnerved him more. "Please...stay...out there."

He paced, waiting for her to emerge. When she finally did, her face was pasty white, her hair wet with perspiration. She held onto the corner of the dresser to balance herself. He rushed to her and, when he would have scooped her off her feet, she stopped him.

"Please, no more sudden movements. My stomach isn't up to it."

Gently, he brushed the wet hair from her cheeks, anchoring it behind her ear, then he caressed her face. "I have to admit, I imagined your response to my declaration of love many ways, but never that way." She didn't smile. "Have you seen a doctor?"

She nodded and ambled toward the bed. Slumping down on the mattress, she leaned her forehead against the wooden post of the footboard. "I saw him yesterday."

"What did he say is wrong?" He put his arm around her shoulders, then gently pulled her head down into the crook of his neck.

She raised her head and smiled at him. "It seems you fulfilled your end of our bargain, but just a few days too late."

"I fulfill—" What she was trying to say suddenly hit him with all the force of a runaway semi. "You're pregnant?"

She nodded, her expression wary. "Do you mind?"

"Mind? Do I mind?" Something very warm and satisfying ebbed through him, filling him with contentment. His child. His wife. He hugged her close. "I couldn't mind less. A baby. Our baby."

She pulled back again and looked at him. "Ah, there's more."

"More?" What more could there be? Was she going to start that stuff about him giving up their child again? "Emily, if you're talking about me leaving and—" She stopped him with a finger to his lips.

"Now, who's jumping to conclusions?"

"If it's about the farm, then I should tell you that I sold my house to Jesse and I used the money to buy the farm from the Horseman's Benevolent Association yesterday. I signed the papers just before I came over here. The farm is yours, Em, forever."

He kissed her lightly. "Of course, you have to take me with it."

Emily's eyes misted. "Oh, Kat. Don't you know I love you? Don't you know I've always loved you, ever since you fell off my roof? Don't you know that living with you, being with you is what's important and not a structure?"

He smiled down at her. In the space of just a few minutes, his every dream had come true. "Then you don't want the farm?"

She kissed him. "I didn't say that. It's just not number one in my life anymore."

"Oh," he grinned down at her, his heart in his eyes. "And what is number one?"

"You. Our babies. Rose. People are what count, not things. I could live anywhere as long as it's with you." Then she laughed. "But I have to admit it is nice to know that we'll be living here where I want my children to grown up."

"Babies. Children. You keep talking in plurals. Can we take this child thing one at a time?"

She shook her head. "Not this time. Rose said twins run in your family. They usually appear every third generation and since she was an only child and you were...."

His contentment deepened to pure joy. "Then we'll have a house full of kids. One at a time or in sets."

She looked deep into his eyes, her face serious, her eyes glowing with her love for him. "There's one other thing this house will be full of."

He kissed the tip of her nose. "What's that?"

"Happiness. And that's a promise."

He believed her, because everyone knew how Emily felt about keeping her promises.

He pulled her close and kissed her. "It's good to finally be home."

Epilogue

Twenty months later

Helping his partner settle in the litter of golden retriever puppies that had just arrived had taken longer than Kat expected. Dr. Grayson had grown so impatient with Kat's hurried movements that he'd finally chased him out of their veterinary office. As he drove, he grinned to himself at Grayson's knowing look as he shooed him from the kennels. Kat considered that opening a veterinary practice with his former college professor had been one of the smartest things he'd ever done—except, of course, for marrying Emily.

Kat swung into the driveway, jumped from the car and then hurried toward the house. He tried hard not to miss this time of day. It had become a ritual that he looked forward to from the time he opened his eyes every morning.

Taking the porch steps in a single bound, he strode into the house, then stopped dead inside the kitchen door. For a long moment, he just stood there drinking in the sight before him. His heart swelled with love and contentment.

Rose and Emily sat on either side of the table. At the side of each woman was a high chair holding one of his twin daughters. Catherine—Cat for short after her daddy—had spinach smeared across her chubby face. Casey, the neater of the two, grinned happily at him.

Lord, would he ever look at these four females and not thank his lucky stars that he'd found them? Would he ever look at his wife and not feel love and passion explode inside him like skyrockets? Would he ever see his mother and not wish for the time together that they'd missed out on? Would he ever see his daughters without thanking God for this tangible proof of his and Emily's love?

Seeing Emily that first day after sixteen long years, she'd stolen his breath, and since then she'd blossomed into the most ravishing woman of his acquaintance. And she was all his, his Emily, his wife.

As if tuning in on his strong emotions, she glanced up and smiled. "You're late."

"Well, I made it in time for dessert." Feeding the girls was something he and Emily had shared from the first day they'd come home from the hospital. He wanted to be as much a part of every aspect of their lives as he could.

Cat pushed away the spoon that Rose had been aiming at her mouth. "Da." She reached her chubby arms out to him.

Rose replaced the spoon in the plastic feeding dish. "I don't know what it is about you that makes these children eat for you and not us, but as long as you're here, see if you can manage to get this child to take some nourishment inside her for a change.'' She stood to give him her chair.

''It's his fatal charm,'' Emily said, shoveling another spoonful of green mush into Casey's open mouth. ''There's not a woman alive who can resist him.''

Laughing, Rose stood on tiptoe and kissed her son's tanned cheek. ''Ain't that the truth. He's his father's son. That's for sure.'' For a moment she just looked up at him, then, running her hand down his arm, she stepped aside.

Ever since the day they'd made peace with each other, Rose seemed to have a need to touch him, to assure herself he was there. Sometimes, even though he never let a day go by without letting her know how much he loved her, he still caught his mother looking at him as if she couldn't believe she'd actually found him again.

''Mom, when are you and my wife going to admit that I'm just better at this than you two are?'' He gave Cat a spoon to occupy her, then, taking the feeding spoon, shoveled a glob of spinach into her mouth. She swallowed and opened wide for more. He shot both women a grin of satisfaction.

Emily wrinkled her nose at him. ''It's got nothing to do with skill.'' She caught Casey's hands just as she was about to check out the peaches with her fingers. ''I don't happen to regard wearing spinach on my clothes as a fashion statement. And I'll have you know, I'm as good at this stuff as you are, Mr. Madison.''

She was. For all Emily's worrying, she'd taken to motherhood like a duck to water. From the day the girls had come home, she'd jumped right into her role with gusto, the same way she did everything in life.

Casey was taking right after her. While Cat, content with the slow pace of crawling to get where she wanted to go, still clung to furniture and had yet to take her first step, Casey had been walking for over a week.

A blinding flash of light interrupted his thoughts. ''I thought by now you'd have enough pictures of your granddaughters.'' He blinked several times to clear away the colored spots dancing across Cat's face.

''I'll never have enough.'' Rose put her always-at-the-ready camera back on the counter. ''Besides, there're still a few empty pages in my album.''

''Which one? Number four or number five?'' Emily grinned at her mother-in-law, then removed Casey from her high chair and set her on her feet on the floor. She toddled unsteadily to her daddy and pounded on his knee with her tiny fist for attention.

As he picked her up and placed her in his lap, Kat skillfully placed the last spoonful of spinach in Cat's mouth, then followed it with a spoonful of peaches. Cat's face screwed up. She sneezed, blowing spinach and peaches all over Casey and Kat. Casey wailed in protest.

"Acts of nature don't count," he told his smug wife above Casey's indignation.

Not saying a word, Emily got a paper towel and cleaned the green and orange polka dots from Casey's and Kat's faces. Casey's cries faded into a series of loud sniffles.

Kat kissed her cheek. "Oh, it's okay, precious. Cat couldn't help it." She treated him to another of her gap-toothed grins.

Emily shook her head, threw the paper towel in the trash, then leaned against the counter and watched her husband with his daughters. *Their* daughters. To think that she had planned on robbing him of all this simply because she was afraid to let her emotions take the lead.

Not long ago, she and Rose had believed themselves, if not totally fulfilled, at least content with their life. Only the last twenty months had shown Emily just how wrong they'd been. Since she'd found Kat's love, her life just continued to get better and better, overflowing with riches of the heart.

If she wanted to be truly honest with herself, even after Kat had settled into her life permanently, there had remained that niggling doubt that he might one day leave again. It wasn't until she came home from the hospital with the twins, and he presented her with a gift he'd made, a matching cradle to the one his grandfather had had made for him, that she'd truly believed he had come home to stay.

She walked to his side and bent to kiss his cheek. "I love you, Mr. Madison," she whispered in his ear.

He grinned that heart-stopping smile of his, then kissed her fingers where they rested lovingly on his shoulder. With his eyes, he made promises for later that brought heat to her cheeks and a familiar lightness to her heart. "Ditto, Mrs. M."

"Later," she promised.

"Date."

"Da!" Cat's demand for more food broke their locked gazes.

The ringing phone snared everyone's attention. The room fell silent as Rose answered it. She spoke softly with her back to them for a few moments, then hung up. Turning to Emily, she sent her a strange look.

"What's up?" Emily's and Kat's voices blended as one.

"It's Honey. She says after you've put the twins down for the night, she needs to talk to you, Emily."

"Why?"

"She was talking very softly, and I couldn't really hear her. It sounded like she said Danny's father's coming home." Rose frowned. "I must have heard wrong. Danny's father's dead." She looked at Emily.

Emily glanced from Rose to Kat. "Not exactly."

Her mother-in-law's mouth dropped open in surprise.

Before either of them could say more, Kat gave Emily a hug, then urged her toward the door.

Emily glanced at him over her shoulder.

"I'm sure Mom misunderstood." He flashed her a we-will-talk-about-this-later look and squeezed her hand. "You'd better get over there and find out what this is all about."

She sent him a grateful smile. "Are you certain you don't want me to help you with their baths?"

Shaking his head, he hoisted Cat from her highchair. "Mom and I can manage just fine."

Grabbing her purse and car keys off a shelf near the back door, Emily threw kisses to everyone. "I'll be back as soon as I can."

Kat winked. "I'll keep the bed warm for you."

She looked at him for a long time, her heart swelling in her chest. How she loved this man, and how she wished Honey could know this kind of happiness. "Promise?"

"Promise."

Since Kat didn't make promises he didn't intend to keep, she knew that, when she returned, she'd find him waiting, arms open wide, to love her far into the night.

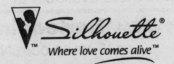

COMING NEXT MONTH

#829 SURPRISE! SURPRISE! by Tina Leonard
Maitland Maternity: Double Deliveries
After months of trying to conceive, Maddie Winston had finally become the
proud mother of twins. But how could she tell her husband, Sam, that she'd
raided his sperm bank "deposit" during their yearlong separation? Would
two bundles of joy be enough to teach Maddie and Sam that love could
overcome all obstacles?

#830 THE RANCHER'S MAIL-ORDER BRIDE by Mindy Neff
Bachelors of Shotgun Ridge
The grizzled matchmakers of Shotgun Ridge, Montana, had found
Wyatt Malone the perfect mail-order bride...without letting the solitary
rancher know. Though Wyatt may not have volunteered for the position,
he was gonna be the first man to help repopulate their little town—whether
he liked it or not!

#831 MY LITTLE ONE by Linda Randall Wisdom
With Child...
Her supposedly innocent blind date had turned into one night to remember!
Though her charming escort, Brian Walker, had saved her from serious
injury and satiated her every need, Gail was certain she'd never see him again.
Until she discovered a little one was on the way....

#832 DOCTOR, DARLING by Jo Leigh
When he unknowingly broke a one-hundred-and-twenty-five-year-old
law, Dr. Connor Malloy was sentenced to take Gillian Bates on a date. But
Gillian was hardly the spinster he expected. How long would it be before the
intelligent beauty had Connor realizing that one night with Gillian wasn't
going to be nearly enough?

Visit us at www.eHarlequin.com

CNM0500